Pippin Pearmain leaves her beloved Lemonwood Cottage in the care of the cats and Cousin Clarkia while she flies to Sydney for her first screen test in decades. A new role, a new agent and a new challenge await, but Pip is sixty-six and she's not sure a comeback is what she wants. Behind her lies a comfortable but eccentric life of performing in offbeat roles, and a decade of living alone. She's short of family and friends, but she has the surprisingly conversational cats, the cottage, and her memories. She has her bucket list and plans for an interesting personal project involving an album and decoupage. Is that enough? Or should she jump feet-first into her new role and see where a comeback takes her?

Pip's few days in Sydney teem with new possibilities, none of which involve decoupage. Mind you, she'll get to that sometime, once she's sorted out two ballets, a film, and a festival.

Performing Pippin Pearmain 4
Copyright © 2023 Lark Westerly
ISBN: 978-1-4874-3715-2
Cover art by Martine Jardin

Published by eXtasy Books Inc

Look for us online at:
www.eXtasybooks.com

Performing Pippin Pearmain 4
Performing Pippin Pearmain

By

Lark Westerly

DEDICATION

For everyone who has a childhood treasure other people don't remember.

Author's Note

Fiction and Reality

Major places in this story, such as Tasmania, the city of Sydney, and the state of Victoria certainly do exist. So does Bass Strait. The towns of Jellico Bay and Delmsford are made up, as is Delphinium Island. The suburb of Windhill with its Fairy Gardens is made up. If it existed, it would be somewhere near North Sydney. Gilchrist would be somewhere near Cremorne. The suburb of Glebe is real as is the iconic Sydney Harbour Bridge. So is the town of Campania. The book Pip remembers in Chapter One is *Dolphin Island,* by Arthur C. Clarke. It was first published in 1963, when Pip would have been eight.

Pip has a screen test in this book. I've never had one of those, so the details may not be accurate. But then, the Diamond Spellman Studio people have a maverick reputation, and they do things their own way. I first wrote about the folks at Diamond Spellman back in the 1990s, telling the story of how Jasper Diamond met Aberdeen Shawcross and how Tasmyn Spellman married Rod Bowen. Revisiting them after so long was fun. I aged them in real time, so Aberdeen and Jasper's daughter, Allirra, who was a small child back then, is now a young woman.

Pip's story covers a year, taking her from her reclusive cottage in Jellico Bay to her old hometown of Delmsford, to the magical fossmere, on to Sydney and thence to Delphinium Island. The nine books compile into one continuing story, slowly revealing the mystery and magic that has been part of

Pip's world all along.

And how did I come to write Pip's story? It all began in February 2022 with a flower show . . . and with a bucket.

The story so far . . .

Book One

Introducing Pippin Pearmain — small, eccentric, determined, sixty-six and ruled by cats. Until a decade ago, Pip earned her living by playing offbeat roles on stage and screen, but after her mother and her agent died in the same week, parts dried up and she moved to Jellico Bay. During a visit to her old hometown she encountered her cousins, Lupin de Leon and Juniper "Jan" Sharman. They, and Jan's daughter, Clarkia, were the only remaining members of the Laurel-Pearmain-de-Leon family. Over afternoon tea at the Delmsford Flower Show, Pip revealed her long-held secret — her bucket list — a literal list of interesting buckets. In return, her cousins wrote down their secrets.

Home in her cottage with the original cat and the back-up cat, which communicate with her in what she thinks of as Cat-Morse, Pip read the secrets. Jan identified herself as the novelist Juniper Gin. Lupin's secret was shocking — she had just a few months to live.

After Lupin's passing, Jan met the cats Kittisack and Amberjill and received a bucket Pip had promised her for Lupin's last repose. They discussed the provenance of a family heirloom — two copies of a book called *Grandmother's Sunshine*. Lacking heirs, Pip had once offered her copy to a young friend, whose mother refused to let her accept it. A call from Jan's daughter prompted Jan to dash off, leaving Pip with Lupin's legacy — an envelope and a pottery cat.

BOOK TWO

Pip received a call from Magda Saxer, announcing herself as Pip's new agent and offering a role in a film called *Half-Life of the Lost*. The cats were unexpectedly in favour. They suggested Jan's daughter would come to look after them.

Lupin's envelope contained a voucher written in disappearing ink. Pip called the information line, whereupon Gerry Trip, Lupin's ex-colleague at Vouch-Safe, informed her she had one hour to prepare for a mystery Experience.

Gerry's step-grandson, Jamie, promised to cat-sit. He drove Pip to a rendezvous.

Pip boarded the yacht *Tulpenmanie*, crewed by pleasant Zach, his odd girlfriend, Jisinia, and Jamie's uncle, Tane.

When Pip realised Tane was missing, she called triple zero. Jisinia confiscated the phone but returned it. Pip rationalised that Tane must have returned to shore.

That night, Tane, who was a silversmith, came back. After resizing a ring for her, he invited Pip to meet his family. She agreed.

Tane picked her up and jumped into the sea.

BOOK THREE

Tane took Pip through an underwater gateway to *over there* where she spent a week with his extended family, practising ballet with Jane and making friends with Tane's spouse, Jillian Jules. The fossmere, a waterfall pool, delighted Pip. She left her tektite ring in the cave behind the falls in gratitude for her adventure. Tane and Jules took her to Hob's Island where she added a new bucket to her list. A sighting of dolphins gave her the idea for a ballet.

Back at Lemonwood Cottage, Pip discovered Jamie, her driver, was a *mutie* or *mutable fay*. He had a second self — a dog he called Kakao.

Jan asked if her daughter Clarkia might come to stay at Lemonwood Cottage while Pip had her screen test.

Book 4, the one you are about to read, begins with a squabble about tea making, takes Pip to Sydney and a film studio, briefly back to the fossmere and into the beautiful Fairy Gardens.

The story continues . . .

PART ONE. SCREEN TEST

April 2022

CHAPTER ONE. TEA OR COFFEE?

It was a decade since Pippin Pearmain had been on a plane, but old habits resurfaced, and she settled into her seat and prepared to tune out the annoying passengers and crew.

That is, she supposed they'd be annoying, and she wasn't prepared to give then the chance to prove it. She glazed over while the flight attendant mimed putting on the life jacket as she indicated the exit rows with a lipstick smile.

Yes, yes, in the event of an emergency we leave all our stuff behind, assume the position, escape via an inflated slide, then bob about in Bass Strait while people paddle out in kayaks to rescue us.

Well, maybe not kayaks.

Maybe dolphins.

She remembered a story she'd loved when she was young. It was about a teenager who was rescued by dolphins when his plane, no, hovercraft, crashed into the sea. He'd been a stowaway, so the escaping crew had no reason to look for him and left him behind.

Better not think of that.

She'd read that ninety-five percent of passengers would theoretically survive a plane crash, but she had no interest in testing it for herself. Figures could lie. For instance, almost everyone could survive a hundred metre fall . . . It was the final few centimetres that did you in.

The plane took off. Pip put on earphones, not because she intended to listen to the in-flight entertainment, but because she wanted to divorce herself as much as possible from the strangers around her.

1

After a while, two attendants came around with a trolley of refreshments.

Tea or coffee? they mouthed, each looking to a different side of the aisle.

"Tea, please," chorused the other two people sharing Pip's row.

Pip watched, appalled, as the left-hand attendant distributed wrapped teabags, sachets of sugar, tiny pots of milk, and ready-poured polystyrene cups of hot water.

"You can't possibly make tea like that!" she blurted.

The attendant stared at her and mouthed, "I beg your pardon?"

Pip removed her earphones. "I said, you can't make tea like that. Tea has to be brewed. If you insist on using teabags, the bags go into the pot or cup. Boiling water, still bubbling, is poured on top. The whole lot is set to brew for at least three minutes. Five is better. You cannot make tea by dipping a tea bag into hot water. It isn't even steaming."

"You mean you would like to unwrap your bag and have me pour water on top?" the attendant clarified.

"No. That water's not boiling. You'd have to do it back in the galley. With boiling water. Or make it in a pot." She'd caught sight of the coffee pot. "You've got coffee in a pot. Surely the least you can do is treat tea-drinkers as well as you treat coffee drinkers! Instant coffee doesn't *need* boiling water. Tea *does*. If you have just one pot, I suggest you make the coffee in cups and use the pot for the tea. It's the only viable solution."

The attendant exchanged baffled glances with her partner.

Pip imagined them saying *Lor' lumme, we got a pain in the arse 'ere, guvnor.*

The right-hand attendant peered round the left-hand one and said, "You're welcome to have coffee, ma'am."

"That's not the point. Anyway, I'll get enough bad coffee on set." Pip considered the cache of camomile tea she had concealed in her luggage. Unfortunately, it was in the hold. And it still required boiling water.

"You'd like tea, then?"

"Yes, if you're prepared to make it properly."

"I'm afraid . . ."

"No need to be afraid. I've explained how to make tea. It's easy. Leaves in the pot or a teabag in the cup. Pour on boiling water and let it steep. A seven-year-old could do it."

"We don't have the facilities . . ."

"Yes you do! Right there." Pip indicated the coffee pot again.

She became aware the other passengers were staring at her with trepidation or distaste. Clearly, what was logical and obvious to her was seen as peculiar and time-wasting and borderline passive-aggressive to them. "Never mind. I'll have water." She couldn't help adding, "I just thought you ought to know how to make tea by now. Didn't your mums teach you?"

One of the attendants passed her a polystyrene cup of water.

Pip thanked him and retreated into her headphones again. Obviously, she shouldn't have said *mums*. She ought to have used the inclusive *parents*, or the even more inclusive *caregivers*. It made her tired.

She had intended to think about the children's dolphin ballet she'd conceived during her recent Experience *over there*, but the ridiculous fuss over teamaking put her out of sorts. It was too late to try sleeping, so she sat in grumpy silence until the plane landed.

Generally, she quite enjoyed people-watching and public eavesdropping, but being cooped up on a plane destroyed the ambiance.

It seemed to take forever for passengers to leave as they opened overhead lockers, shuffled forwards, half rose to their feet and subsided again, and got their over-sized cabin baggage wedged in the inadequate aisle.

Pip reverted to her usual trick of staying seated until there was room to move without being squashed by someone's large shoe.

"Is everything all right, ma'am?" One of the attendants bent to look at her.

"Yes thanks. I'm waiting for a chance to get out without being flattened in the stampede."

"I think there's room now," the attendant said politely. "Shall I help you?"

It was the left-hand tea-server.

Pip sighed. "Sorry about the tea. It's just . . ." She almost gave up. "I suppose you're *not* a tea-drinker yourself?"

The attendant smiled. "No, ma'am. I'm a coffee-drinker."

"Then I shouldn't expect you to understand."

"I'm—"

"Listen, I've thought of another analogy. Have you ever made instant porridge?"

The attendant nodded.

"Have you ever made quick oats?"

"Probably."

"Do you know the difference?"

The attendant seemed to be thinking. Finally, he said, "I think one is ready when you pour water over it and let it sit. The other one needs to be cooked, but it doesn't take long."

"Right. Instant porridge is similar to instant coffee. Quick oats is more like tea. You can pour hot water over quick oats, but it will just taste like hot, wet raw oats. Understand?"

The attendant glanced along the body of the plane. "Ma'am, they're waiting to clean the plane. May I be of any further assistance?"

"I can manage." Pip slid out of the seat and looked up at the overhead locker. "If you could just—"

The attendant, who stood a good quarter metre taller than Pip's 149 cm, obligingly retrieved her overnight case.

Pip turned it end-wise and left the plane. She had done her best. The attendant had been unfailingly civil and attentive, but she knew he hadn't understood. Or—maybe he had understood but was unable or unmotivated to do anything to remedy the situation.

The airport was every bit as busy as she remembered, with crowds of people and the occasional beeping indoor vehicle for those with low mobility.

Rather than wander blindly, Pip asked an attendant from another gate where the flights from Western Australia came in. She collected her case from the carousel and found a café near the designated gate where she ordered cambric tea.

They did have camomile on the menu, but she knew from experience that it wouldn't taste like hers.

The barista had never heard of cambric tea.

Pip wanted to fling her hands up, but instead she ordered weak tea with lots of milk and hoped for the best.

Soy latte?

No! Cambric tea! With tea off a camellia sinensis bush, and milk out of an actual cow. Not soy. Not gluten free. Not decaffeinated. Tea!

Chapter Two. Magda

Pip was still waiting for her tea when a tall woman stalked up to her table in a flurry of black and brilliant colours. "You'll be Pippin Pearmain."

Pip got up from the table and looked into a fierce handsome face crowned with thick white hair in an improbable milkmaid braid. The woman wore a dark calf-length dress with a multicoloured embroidered shawl and sturdy brogues.

"There's not much of you, is there?" she observed, looking down at Pip.

"There's enough," Pip riposted. "Magda, right?"

"Yes. Let's see." She stepped back and gave Pip the once-over. "You haven't changed a lot."

"Since when?" Pip was sure they hadn't met before.

"Since *The Girl in the Frame*. That was your latest role, right?"

"Yes." Pip frowned. She had few good memories of that film shoot. She had never actually met the other actors. The director, or *facilitator* as he liked to call himself, had been a slippery character named Wayne Ellington. Sully hadn't cared for him either. Pip thought it a pity her last job with Sully had been that one. The others had been fun.

Escapades, Sully liked to call them.

Magda went on looking her over. "I'd almost say you haven't changed at all. I expected you to look older. Had some work done?"

"I had a little holiday last week, but I haven't had *work* done, if you mean what I think you mean. Does it matter?"

"No. The part you're up for doesn't call for a particular age . . . it's more about presence and the ability to sell the character. Good flight?"

"Not very."

Magda snorted. "They never are. Waste of time, if you ask me. Never fly if I can help it. Haven't flown in five years."

"I thought you said you were landing half an hour after me."

"Doubt it. Maybe I said I'd get in half an hour after . . . never mind. We're both here now. Let's go."

"I'm still waiting for my tea," Pip objected.

"I shouldn't bother. Bound to be horrible." She turned and swept out of the café, where she was intercepted by a woman with black hair going grey, a charmingly crooked mouth, and the brightest green eyes Pip had ever seen in anyone but a cat. Pip judged her to be a bit younger than herself, but it was difficult to tell.

"For God's sake, Magda! Can't leave you alone for five minutes! Now what have you done?"

Magda indicated Pip, then nodded to the other woman. "Pippin Pearmain, meet Pandora Inkersoll. Panda, this is Pip, the asset."

Pandora Inkersoll raised a brow at Pip. "Hello, asset. I'm your chauffeur *pro tem*. Is that all your luggage?"

"Yes," Pip said. "Call me Pip."

"Okay. Call me Panda if you like. Most people do. It saves rude quips about *boxes*." She grinned. "I've put you in a guesthouse run out of a Victorian terrace house. Nicer than a motel, by far." She led the way out of the airport to a van. "Hop in." She opened the side door, and Pip caught a whiff of a familiar scent—the sweet-sharp tang of crushed lemon leaves.

Magda got in beside Pip. "I know I said taxi and motel, but Panda offered to organise things. She lives in these parts, so I took her up on it. Knew she'd do a good job. Her dad's a *very*

7

old client of mine."

"I've told you a hundred and one times Peter is *not* my dad," Pandora said as she pulled out into the traffic. "Jacobi's my dad, bless him. Peter might have planted me, but Jacobi has loved me and cared for me all my life."

"Yes, yes, I know the spiel. Proper dads are rare, and you've got two of them." Magda added to Pip, "My friend Peter P had a wee slip-up with Panda's mum back in the day. She rushed off and married Jacobi. Let's be clear, Jacobi knew about the proto-Pandora in the pot when he married Barbie. Peter was such a green lad he had no idea until years and years later."

"Mag-da! Miss Pearmain doesn't want to know my murky history."

"It's not your murky history, dear. It's theirs. And it's not so very murky. Everyone behaved well, though your mum *should* have told Peter P." Magda turned to Pip. "Peter P lives down at the tower near Patterdale in Victoria, and the le Fays are mostly up here in Windhill or thereabouts. I'm at Tom Cat Hill in Western Australia, so the affair would have stayed decently under wraps if Panda hadn't wandered into Magdala Gallery one time in the seventies. I had some choice limited edition prints of the *Swansong* tryptic on the wall, starring Peter P in his rather wonderful bare hide as the swan and a waifish young woman called Judit Creed as Leda. You know the story of Leda and the Swan?"

"I do," Pip said cautiously.

"Peter P looked human in it, sort of, but magnificently *other*. The artist, also an old friend — though we never met in person — was an old soak, but he had an eye for colour and composition that would make you weep."

"Who was he?" Pip asked with interest.

"Thaddeus Bellover Appledore. He died when he should have been making a magnificent comeback — the drink got him." She sniffed.

Pip was unfamiliar with this artist, but she thought she might look him up when she got home.

Magda continued, "One look at Panda here, when she walked into my gallery, and I knew for a fact from whose loins *she'd* sprung. The resemblance is unmistakable. I'd have said Peter P was a one-off, but Panda's practically his clone. Barbie's genes are nowhere. Barbie's your classic blue-eyed blondie, you see. Classy, mind you . . . none of that brassy trash. She's tall and wholesome-looking with a nice figure, like a sixties sit-com mum." She paused, apparently musing. "Grey now, of course, but it's not so obvious with blondes."

Panda interrupted Magda's spiel. "Magda. That really is enough. Do I need to ask Davey's dad to have a *word* regarding the milk of human kindness and the evils of gossip?"

"Right. Heaven forefend that you sool the old red cat on me." Magda clammed up and Pip looked out the window, trying to collect her thoughts. Leda and the Swan was one of the more scandalous Greek myths, she thought, unless it was Roman. Leda had been Helen of Troy's mother.

With those facts safely recalled, she moved on to thinking about Magda herself.

Magda had claimed a long-standing friendship with Sullivan "Sully" Gilbert, who had been Pip's agent for nearly fifty years, and Pip sort of saw how that might have worked. Both women were forthright and outspoken, but Sully had been like family — a kind of guardian aunt who organised things. Magda was like Sully cubed and on steroids, and she and Pip had no long, shared history to soften their edges.

Pip realised she was used to being the most outspoken person in the room — especially now Cousin Lupin had gone to glory. Then she reflected on Jisinia from the yacht *Tulpenmanie*, and Tane, Sam and Jules and the rest of the family at the fossmere. Some of them were devastatingly frank. Even darling Jane had suggested she looked salty and bedraggled when they first met.

To be fair, it was true. Jane had mentioned it in one breath and offered some generous and practical solutions in the next.

She decided to appreciate Magda's directness, but not to encourage her.

There was no way she and Magda could enjoy a fifty-year association as she and Sully had, but the next day or so might give her a clearer indication of whether they worked as a team. If they did, it would be good for them both. If not—they could formally part company. It wouldn't be difficult. She'd thought her career was over anyway. She was old enough to retire if she chose.

Pandora drove over the bridge and on into Glebe. She pulled up in a quiet street of Victorian terrace houses. "Here we are. This place is run by the Treadwell family, Pip. Joan and Edgar are the current managers. Just ask either of them for anything you want, and they'll do their best for you. Joan is fun, and she's a terrific cook. Edgar's a darling, your favourite uncle and an old-time porter rolled into one."

"I want camomile tea," Pip said.

"That should be easy. Edgar grows herbs over near the castle. He's got green fingers."

She got out and opened the sliding side door so Pip and Magda could disembark. A knock at the door brought a genial-looking giant to take their cases. "This is Edgar," Pandora said as the giant engulfed Pip's hand in his enormous paw. "Edgar, you know Magda already, and this is Pippin Pearmain." To Pip, she added, "Okay? I'll pick you up tomorrow and drive you to Diamond Spellman."

"Hello, lass," Edgar growled, giving Pip's hand a gentle squeeze.

"Diamond Spellman is the studio where you get the screen test," Magda said. "Dunno why—but it's where the client said to go. G'day, Edgar . . . how goes it with the Treadwell den?"

"Doing well, Missus Saxer. Our Davina birthed another cub, so t' line is well represented in the new generation."

"No need for the *Missus Saxer* business. You call Torkel by his first name, so you can do the same for me."

"Magda." Edgar let go of Pip and took Magda's hand.

"I'll see you at ten," Pandora said. "Ed—"

"I'll behave myself, lass. Dunno about Miss Pearmain. She looks like a knowing one to me."

Pip, fed up with travel, just wanted to go to a quiet room and realign herself. She followed Edgar and Magda up two flights of steps. They were worn and steep, so she was glad Edgar had taken possession of the heavier bags.

"You're in here, Miss Pearmain," Edgar said in his gruff voice, stopping on a landing. He put down her bag and opened a door, letting her enter before he followed with the bag. "If you want anything at all, let one of us know and we'll whistle it up."

"Do you have lemons?" Pip asked.

"Aye. We grow them in the courtyard."

"Do you pee on the trees?"

He laughed. "That I do."

"Good." She looked around her temporary domain. "This looks comfy, but—"

"But?" Magda stepped in to join them. She sounded disapproving.

"I need a space big enough for me to do my morning ballet practice without disturbing anyone. Not in here, obviously, but maybe you have a common room or something?"

Edgar glanced at Magda. "Does it have to be a room? There's the courtyard out t' back, and if that's not big enough I can let you through to a big stretch of turf beyond t' gate."

"That'll do perfectly," Pip said.

"What time would that be?"

11

"I start at seven o'clock."

Magda shook her head. "No wonder you look so revoltingly fit. Edgar, if you go through the gate will you stay to bring her safely back? Or get Joan to? Don't want my asset wandering off."

Pip bristled, but Edgar said placidly, "I'll do it, lass, don't worry. One last thing, Miss Pearmain—"

"Pip."

"Pip. It's dinner time, so will you come to the dining room once you've settled in, or would you rather have a tray? No trouble to us."

"A tray please," Pip said gratefully.

The man nodded. "Twenty minutes. You have a kettle and teapot, and I'll send up t' tea and t' lemon."

He and Magda departed, and Pip flopped onto the bed. The room was comfortable, with an armchair upholstered to match the pretty curtains embroidered with flowers and sprigs of wheat.

Pip was briefly reminded of Little Mum's rose-upholstered rocking chair. The coffee stain it had acquired on the day Sully died hadn't come out, but she *could* have had it re-covered in similar fabric. She wished she had. Instead, she'd left it behind with all the other furnishings at *Treasures,* the parental home where she had lived until Little Mum's passing. That chair would have fitted beautifully in Lemonwood Cottage. She supposed she might get another one, but it wouldn't be the same.

No good trying to get back what I've lost. Better consider what I have.

She thought wistfully of Lemonwood Cottage and the cats. She'd left them just a handful of hours ago, but they seemed curiously distant.

Well ... she could connect with them now. Before she could second-guess herself, she brought up Cousin Clarkia's new number on her phone and hit the green button.

"Pip?" Clarkia sounded doubtful.

"Yes. Didn't my name come up?"

"No. I'll have to put you in memory."

"Do that. I've got to where I'm staying, and I called to see if everything's okay."

"Oh — fine. Lovely, in fact. I'm having dinner with four eyes staring at me."

"That's normal." She didn't mention Lupin's cat. "Don't let them con you into believing they're starved. And if you don't want them on the bed — "

"They're welcome if that's what they want. It's their house. They're good company."

"Yes, they are." Pip wondered if she should enlighten Clarkia as to the cats' provenance, but she decided not to. If they wanted her to know, they'd tell her themselves. Not that they'd ever told *her*, until she confronted them with it, but they hadn't exactly tried to hide the ways in which they diverged from what Pip thought of as cat-normal.

"Anyway . . . I'm glad everything's well. Just let me know if you can't find anything. I'll answer if I can, but my phone will be off at the studio."

"I'll text rather than ring. Are you staying somewhere nice?"

"Yes. It's a terrace house not far off Glebe Point Road. I'm up two flights of steps in a cosy room with everything I need and nothing I don't."

"No wide-screen telly with a theatre chair and holders for your popcorn, then?"

"No telly at all."

Clarkia, Pip noted, didn't say anything either sympathetic or dismissive about televisions. That was tactful of her, considering how Pip had made her living.

"Nice view?"

"Um . . ." Pip moved across to open the curtains. "It's dark,

13

so it's hard to say. I'm looking down at a courtyard, I think. It's not the street. This is a pretty quiet area anyhow, with lots of trees."

"That sounds lovely."

There was a small pause, then Clarkia added, "Goodnight, Pip. Thank you for giving me a refuge."

The short conversation left Pip feeling curiously unsettled. She'd felt bad that she couldn't properly share Jan's grief over Lupin's passing, but at least she had experience with losing loved ones to death. Six grandparents, since Big Nanna and Big Pop de Leon had always treated her the same way as they treated Jan and Lupin, had gone from her life, followed by Jan and Lupin's dad, her own darling Little Dad Jon, Aunt Helen, and finally Little Mum Rosie. Sully's abrupt death three days later during a supportive visit to Pip had added to the grief. She at least understood a bit of how Jan felt over Lupin, and she also felt the unfairness of Lupin's passing at seventy. Judging by the family statistics, she should have had at least fifteen years more.

Clarkia's grief was another thing entirely. How on earth did it feel to love and invest in someone for four years, then face abrupt but long-term betrayal? It appeared Clarkia hadn't seen or even spoken with her deceptive boyfriend since the revelation of his double life, so her last physical memory of him was probably an affectionate hug and kiss, or a smiling *see you when I see you* as he left on one of what she believed to be his regular business trips.

Pip didn't know the full story because everyone told their tales from their own perspective, but, as Clarkia said, there seemed no doubt of his duplicity. He'd told her his children would barely recognise him, and that their mother had cut ties with him when they were small. His girlfriend had implied they were still together when he wasn't *on the road* and had shown photos to prove a close and ongoing association.

Photos could be falsified, but according to Clarkia these had been casual snaps. In one of them, his look-alike daughter had been sitting on his lap with her arm around his neck. She'd looked around nine years old. Difficult to doctor that kind of thing.

How had he kept the secret for four years? Surely Clarkia and the other woman sometimes called him when he was away? Maybe not. Maybe he insisted on texts or turned down his phone when he was *at home* in either place. It would be easy to claim he didn't want to be disturbed by persistent work colleagues while at *home* or distracted by personal calls when at *work*. Apart from her parents' long and devoted marriage, Pip had little idea of how couples managed their communications when apart. Little Dad and Little Mum had rarely been parted . . . except in the early years when Little Mum used to go with Sully and Pip when Pip had a job. Even then, Little Dad had often accompanied them or paid visits to the set.

That was long before mobile phones, but Pip was sure they'd spoken on the landline most days. And 1960s landlines, unlike modern mobiles, required one to be where one was supposed to be.

Big Nanna and Big Pop de Leon had spent regular holidays apart, but they'd been on close and loving terms in between times.

She shrugged and sighed. At least the cats were flourishing.

And she had access to lemon and water and the promise of a suitable place for dancing in the morning. *A big stretch of turf,* Edgar had called it. That put her in mind of the flat dancing ground at Fosscot, although obviously it would lack a helpful young musician who could play anything by ear. She had her phone with its stored music library. Things could certainly be worse.

CHAPTER THREE. BALLET AT THE CASTLE

The morning ballet practice ran into a hitch when Pip discovered her phone wouldn't work.

She couldn't understand it. It was fine when she checked the weather ap at half past six, but after Edgar escorted her out to the courtyard and put a hand on her shoulder to usher her through a back gate into what she assumed was the promised park, it presented a blank screen.

"Dammit!"

"Anything wrong, lass?" Edgar asked.

"My phone's gone dead." She drew in a deep breath of the clear, bracing air. It was difficult to believe she was in a major city, though, as she'd told Clarkia, it was a leafy suburb.

"We're out of range of t' signal. I can take you back through to t' terrace if you want to make a call."

"I don't want to make a call. I want to play my practice music. I don't suppose *you* have dance music on your phone?" she said without much hope. He didn't look like the kind of man who enjoyed portable ballet music.

He shook his head. "Out o' range for me, too." Then he brightened. "Got a mouth organ, if that'll do?"

"I suppose . . . what can you play?"

"Lass, what *can't* I play?" He fished in the pocket of his loose shirt. "How about a bit of a waltz? Joan's always been partial to a waltz. Used to play to her when we were courting. Still do." He chuckled, sounding like gravel in a barrel. "Had to do summat to persuade t' lass I knew how to romance her." He ticked off on his fingers. "Askin,' bakin,' cuddlin' an' dancin.' That's the courtin' ABC. Mind, it does just as nicely for t' marriage afterwards."

"Thanks." Pip was unsure how to respond to that comment, so she went for general appreciation. There was no barre, but she started limbering up, doing centre exercises to music in her mind.

Edgar seated himself on a bank . . . or possibly a step . . . played an introductory trill, then swung into a waltz Pip didn't know. Not to worry, it had a good regular cadence, and the instrument had a clear tone, so she settled in to work.

Edgar was as good a musician as he'd implied. He segued into another tune, then another, unfamiliar, but fitting the rhythm of dance like a glove. He put in trills and syncopation sometimes, keeping her literally on her toes. Then came a tune she knew.

"Silk and Circumstance" was an old friend, and she'd recently become reacquainted with it while practising with Jane.

Gradually, as the movements became automatic, she started to notice her surroundings. She was on a flat stretch of turf rimmed with a slope, and she spotted gardens over to one side.

She was pretty sure she'd never been to this part of Sydney before, but she experienced a strong feeling of déjà vu. Her steps faltered, but she caught herself up, drawing in the clear air.

The grass was short and the ground forgiving, so she ran through the dolphins' entry with some travelling *jetes*. As she came to the end of the sequence, Edgar brought the music to a close. "How long do you need, Miss Pip?"

"I usually do an hour . . ."

He laughed. "You've been at it for longer than that, and Mistress Inkersoll is picking you up at ten."

Someone applauded behind her, and Pip turned abruptly

to see a young woman watching them. She had long blonde hair and a white dress and carried an old-fashioned marketing basket over one arm.

Seeing Pip had stopped dancing, she came over. "Greet you this fine morning, Edgar. Who's your friend?"

"I'm Pippin Pearmain," Pip said. Feeling some explanation might be needed, she added, "At home, I do my practice every morning at seven. I don't want to miss out while I'm here. My phone went flat, so Edgar offered to play for me instead. He's better than the music library."

The young woman said, "You can always rely on Edgar to do what's wanted. Joan, too. If she can't do something, she's bound to know someone who can. What was that you were dancing? I know the tune, of course, but I didn't recognise the ballet sequence."

"It's the opening of *Delphine* . . . the entry of the dolphins," Pip said. She hadn't known until then that her ballet was to be called *Delphine,* but it seemed appropriate.

"Ah, that explains the leaps." She nodded approval. "Have to look that one up . . . Joyful—that's my little girl—loves dancing. She's three, but she already seems to have some structure to her movement, rather than aimlessly jiggling and skipping around the way most children her age do. Best be off . . . just making a delivery to the kitchens." She indicated off to the side, smiled and walked on.

Pip frowned, turning. In the middle distance, she saw an imposing building she almost recognised.

Can't be.

She glanced at Edgar. "This is going to sound silly, but exactly where are we?"

He said, "Summer Court, some call it, or just t' castle. Young Felicity trained as a confectioner here and she still does a bit o' work for t' castle folk. She and her man run a café in Sydney otherwise. The Dark Room, they call it, on account of their surname being Dark."

He indicated a stone structure down the slope. "That over there's the castle bridge."

Pip opened her mouth and closed it. She looked round again. Then she said, "We're not in Sydney anymore, are we."

Edgar gave a smile and a tiny shrug. "Nay . . . but you can be back there in a minute or so whenever you give the word."

"I see." She stared at the castle. She'd not seen it from this angle before, but she was sure it was the one Jane's friend Ardal Cornfellow had pointed out when he took her riding up in the chalklands.

But this place is near Sydney. I came in via Bass Strait.

Ah! So that explains why my phone is dead!

She remembered Jules explaining that phones, electricity and batteries didn't work *over here* in the fay homeland. Why hadn't Edgar said that when she mentioned her flat phone? Either it was self-evident to him, or else he'd hoped she might think she was just in a park that happened to be near the guesthouse.

She shook her head and focused on Edgar, who was polishing his mouthorgan on his voluminous shirt. There was no point in challenging him. He had done nothing wrong. He'd done as she asked, brought her somewhere suitable for dancing, and provided her with the wherewithal to do it.

"Is this where you grow your herbs?" she asked politely.

His smile broadened. "It is, aye. There's not much room in the courtyard, so I use a big plot around t' back there. The folk at t' castle don't mind. They know they can help themselves. Herbs need picking. It's their reason for being grown. Flick — Felicity that is — does too, and she brings honey to Joan for the parkin as a fair exchange." He pursed his lips. "Most folk use treacle, and so does Joan, but she halves it with ginger honey. I grow ginger, see, and Flick's bees are partial to it."

Pip gave up on trying to process that. "I *thought* that camomile tea was extra good. If it was home grown, that explains it. Are you a hob, Master Treadwell?"

"I am that, but I was born in Merimbula. Our branch of the family *lives human* as they say." He got up from what she now identified as a mossy step cut into the rising ground. "Best be getting back to t' terrace, or Joan'll be after me with the frying pan." His following chuckle suggested he either wasn't serious or else enjoyed a little altercation.

CHAPTER FOUR. DIVIDENDS

Pip was gratified to find a squeezed lemon in a covered cup in her room. She boiled her kettle while she showered and contemplated her situation through the vapour.

Edgar Treadwell, and presumably his wife Joan, were hobs. She'd met two male hobs during her holiday at the fossmere — William Cliff and Ardal Cornfellow. She might add Jamie Pendennis to the list since he had a hob grandfather, although he'd denied having any major hob tendencies . . . whatever they were.

So what, precisely, was a hob? Why did they all — except for Jamie — show traces of Yorkshire in their speech? Edgar said he was born in Merimbula, which she understood to be on the Sapphire Coast, well south of Sydney. He ought to talk like a New South Welshman.

The family at the fossmere had been a blend of pisky, waterfolk, and sylvan with a few human genes tossed into the mix via Jillian Jules' flower child of a mother, and a whole lot more variations through Mama Tam's quest for beautifully assorted children. Pip had met at least two pure leprechauns and some halflings, but she'd never pinned anyone down and got them to explain exactly what it all meant in detail. There should be a loose inclusive term for them all . . . fairies? Fay? They must belong to the same general genetic pile as humans because they happily intermarried and produced melting pot children.

She might ask Jamie, but he wasn't exactly a goldmine of information. She'd practically had to hold him down to extract information about his inner dog, Kakao.

The cats? She recalled Tam mentioning *fay cats,* so maybe the people *over there* could confidently be termed *fay.* That would work. Kittisack and Amberjill were cats, and she was finally convinced they were visible and corporeal for others than herself, but they were not quite ordinary cats. They were fay cats. She'd put it to them, and they hadn't denied it.

Crikey! What if they decide to breed! Pip hastily put the thought away. Amberjill was the original cat's apprentice. *Surely* he wouldn't. Eek! But if they did . . . and who was she to decide who might and might not procreate . . . she'd have some fascinating new companions.

I need an encyclopaedia . . . a sensible one. Might ask Edgar. He said I could ask for what I want, so I darned well will.

With that decision made, she turned off the taps, pressed water out of her hair and wrapped herself in a towel.

Where's Mama Tam with her patent hair drying magic method when I need her?

It occurred to her that she might be able to pay the fossmere family a visit while she was in Sydney — if she could remember the way from the castle. Maybe Edgar would take her.

Not now. Got to get ready for that screen test.

Fairly dry and dressed in the neat and practical costume Sulane had given her, Pip drank her lemon and water and ate the breakfast someone had left for her while she showered.

It included a ginger cake she hesitatingly identified as the parkin Edgar had extolled, as well as stewed pears and a boiled egg with brown bread and butter. It was not what she'd usually eat, but it made a pleasant change. There was a small pot of camomile tea, delicately painted with white camomile flowers and their ferny leaves.

For a moment she flashed on Lupin's cat, with his decorative pattern of purple lupins and green leaves. The glaze was the same, but Cousin Lupin couldn't possibly have made this.

She held the pot up to admire it and spotted a maker's

mark of an oval in which stood a figure in a shepherd's smock holding a giant stalk of corn.

Cornfellow.

Smiling, she wondered if Jane's Ardal had set his hand to making this pot. He'd said he worked at *t' pottery*.

At a quarter to ten, Pip presented herself downstairs, where she encountered Edgar in a big kitchen.

She cleared her throat to let him know she was there, and he froze for a few seconds before turning to face her. "Lass, you startled me."

"Sorry. Magda and I are going out shortly, but you *said* I could ask for anything I needed."

"Go ahead. Phone chargers, combs, sun hats, calculators, a tame gazelle, troll under t' bed . . ."

"My phone's okay now I'm back human-side. What I wanted to know is if there's an encyclopaedia I could borrow."

"There's an old one Joan and I got for t' children, but it'd be out of date."

"No, I meant one describing your people. About the — the *fay*." She brought out the term more in hope than in certainty, but Edgar's broad face creased into a grin.

"There is that! I'll look it out for you. Joan and I have signed copies."

"Oh?"

"The author has connections round here — a couple of cousins. You met one after your dancing."

"The blonde girl?"

"Felicity Dark. The author did a few interviews and such round these parts, and t' wife and I got the books as a thank-thee."

Pip perceived the fay world was much wider than she'd thought. "I'd love to look at them while I'm here," she ventured. Then, recalling what she'd said to Jan regarding buying her book series rather than borrowing them, she added, "Of course I'm equally happy to buy my own if they're in the local shops. If not, I could probably order it from *The Orange Grove.*"

Edgar nodded placidly. "Best look at ours first — make sure they're what you were wanting. Buy later if they are."

"I will. Thank you."

A knock on the outer door and Magda's arrival downstairs brought her purpose for being in Sydney crashing back into Pip's mind.

Screen test. Why? They've surely seen me in earlier roles. But — I'm older now.

Pandora Inkersoll ushered her and Magda into her van. "Got everything?"

Pip patted her pockets and her messenger bag. "Let's hope so."

Magda looked her over. "Did you bring any costume changes?"

"No." Sully had always taken care of that. "I could get something out of my bag upstairs."

"Humph. Silly question. Wouldn't fit much into that shoulder bag contraption. Never mind. They'll likely have something —"

"I haven't seen the sides yet."

"Doubt if you will. I gather it's ad-lib."

What?

"You can do that?" Magda prompted.

"I did natural reaction — or was it logical moves — in *Girl in the Frame,*" she allowed.

"There you go, then." Magda assessed her again. "No battle paint."

"No."

"Good. Save 'em taking it off you. Don't know what they're planning — ghostly pallor or what. Your skin's good."

"I use Caraway's Comforts lotions every day. I also indulge in camomile tea, lemon juice and water, daily ballet practice, and strawberries and cream," Pip said promptly.

"Sounds sensible to me," Magda said. "Plus whiskey now and again. You?"

"Not usually," Pip said.

"Probably wise, given your — "

"Size. Yes."

"I should have asked you before — do you have any particular ritual before you do a test? Lucky charms? Meditation?"

Pip recalled her heaven and earth ring. That was a lucky charm of sorts, a gift from Sully. It was now in a rock niche at the back of the fossmere.

Still bringing me luck. Now I know I can go back for a visit. I have my passport to fairy land.

She patted her messenger bag, where the ring had lived in its little soft pouch.

I've still got the . . . other thing. Maybe that could move into the pouch.

But the *other thing* was so private and so precious she had never mentioned it to *anyone* and barely ever thought of it. Putting it in the heaven and earth ring's pouch might bring it to the universe's attention.

She said, "No rituals. I just go on and do what they ask for."

"That's surprisingly untemperamental of you."

Pip said, "I'm not temperamental when it comes to performing. I told you before, I never studied acting, though I've taken ballet classes and learned fan dancing and fencing and rope climbing for different roles."

"Fascinating," Magda said.

"Not really. It was the *thing* in the sixties and early seventies. You learned ballet, or gymnastics, or riding, or photography, or went birdwatching, or played sport. No tablets or computers or mobiles. I just did things associated with my roles. Ballet's the one that stuck. You know what they say. *The best exercise is the one you* do."

Magda nodded. "What else did you do?"

Pip considered. "Aside from ballet? Whatever I needed to be able to do. I read a lot. Big Nanna de Leon used to take us on holiday to interesting places."

"Who was *us?*"

"My cousins—Lupin and Juniper de Leon and me. Mum and Aunt Helen were twins who stayed close, so we grew up with functionally six grandparents."

"Are your cousins performers?"

Lupin. Pip stubbed her toe on sorrow. She said, "Lupin was older than me. She was headmistress at the *Mary Shelley* school until she retired. After that, she worked for Vouch-Safe for a while. Do you know of that company?"

"I do."

"I thought you might. She went to glory a couple of weeks ago . . . I hadn't seen her or Jan—that's Juniper—for a decade or so because I'd moved away, but I ran into them at the flower show back in February. I hoped we'd catch up more often, but it was too late for Lupin."

"It's hard losing family, even if you haven't seen them in a while—or ever."

Pip wondered who Magda had lost, but she didn't ask. At her age, whatever it really was, she'd probably lost most of them.

"Jan's two years younger than me . . .born six years after Lupin. She's a novelist. She writes under a pen name—Juniper Gin."

"That's your only family?"

"Jan and I are the only ones left of the whole three families in the Laurel-de Leon-Pearmain clan, aside from Jan's daughter Clarkia, who's cat-sitting for me. I hadn't seen *her* in years. I don't remember if she was at my mother's funeral, which was the last time we all got together . . . until February, I mean." She frowned. "They didn't come to Sully's funeral. Did you?"

Magda said, "Eventually. I'm not good with funerals. I only got to my mum's because Peter P braced me up with spirits and love." She paused and called forward, "Stop bristling, Panda. It wasn't *that* sort of love. Pia would have had me on toast if it had been."

Pandora said, "I don't care *who* my original father loves. Pia's welcome to him."

"You ought to care. You've got his blood in your veins. Damned fine blood it is, too."

Pandora took that one in silence.

After a bit, Magda said, "I got to Sully's send-off eventually, and raised a glass of Fagus Ale to her with a Tom Cat Hill Whiskey chaser. Torkel came to keep me company, and to monitor my libations. Sometimes I suspect he's in league with Peter P to keep me sober."

Torkel?

Pip remembered Magda mentioning that name to Edgar. She said, "That explains why I didn't see you there. I don't drink—much—so I went to the service and skipped the wake."

Magda switched the subject slightly. "I have some experience of being the only one left. My father died in the Spanish flu epidemic before I was born. He and my mother weren't married, and she left me with my grandmother while she went home to break the news to her parents that they had a grandchild. She never came back. I don't know if she had an accident, died in the epidemic, or just decided I was a burden she didn't want to shoulder. Or maybe her parents threatened to disown her if she brought me home."

Pip winced. "Ouch."

"Not for me. I had no idea of any of this until I was well and truly past caring. I grew up with my grandmother, whom I called *Mum,* and her husband. She married *him* partly to give me a father figure, and it worked out beautifully. It wasn't until Mum was in her nineties that she told me the truth. Of course I had no idea she was anything like so old. She didn't look it."

"I'm surprised no one told you before. Back in the day people used to *love* telling that sort of news. These days . . . who cares?"

"Nobody knew there was anything to tell. Even Philip, Mum's husband, might not have known. He was a lovely man, older than Mum, I think . . . or maybe not. On second thoughts, he must have known *something*, because he always referred to me as Magda, or *our girl,* rather than introducing me as his daughter or stepdaughter. I called him Pips, not Dad."

"Really? Pips?"

Magda cackled. "His name was Philip, and he had carroty hair. Orange-pips, see?" She paused and said, "Oh, I see what you mean. You're a Pippin, and he was a Philip, though. The names aren't all that close, and not a bit alike in meaning. Anyway, he took Mum's family name, and I still don't know what his original one was."

And I thought our family was odd!

"No cousins?" Pip asked.

"Not to my knowledge. My father, Wilhelm, was an only child, and as I said, he died before I was born. My mother — no idea. All I really know of her is her first name, Francine. When she didn't come back for me, Mum tried to get in touch with her at the address she'd given, but her letters were returned *not known.* That might have meant she had never lived there at all, or that she'd been disowned anyway, or even that the family just didn't want to be contacted. I don't know what the address was. Mum hadn't kept it, and I have no idea if she ever tried to find out more. I didn't know any of this until just before Mum died."

She paused, and said in a different tone, "I've only got Mum's testimony for all this, you understand . . . and a photo of Wil and Francine . . . but she was a truthful person, on the whole, and she knew she was going to go to glory. She'd always done her best for me. Why would she make up stories?"

"I can't see why she would," Pip said, although Clarkia's boyfriend, whose name she still didn't know, had undoubtedly done that. "It's you on your own, then," she added with a flash of fellow feeling.

"Not exactly. I never expected to marry, but after Mum went, there were things I couldn't do for myself. She had a *knack,* you see. I was lonely, so I took in short-term boarders. That was Peter P's suggestion when he came to support me at Mum's funeral. Got a good head on him, has Peter P."

"Why Peter P?" Pip put in.

"Old story. He's an only child, called Peter Peckerdale. He has a cousin who's also a Peter — well, Salix Peter — with the surname Grene. Since both used *Peter* for their forename, they became known as Peter P and Peter G."

A grumpy sound came from the front seat, and Magda abandoned the subject of her old client.

"One boarder I took in was a lovely kid — Idonea. Her dad used to come and visit her at my place, to make sure she was okay, and not fretting, as he said. Not that she ever did! After a bit, I noticed he'd come to visit and stay on even when she was off with her friends. He was on his own and so was I, so in the end we tied the knot. I didn't lose out on her rent since she paid me in kind rather than money. Torkel and I even managed a daughter of our blood. Big surprise *she* was! I thought I was way too old to have a child."

Pip reflected on Jillian Jules, who was in her sixties and who had an unweaned baby.

"What's your daughter's name?"

"Marianna, after Mum. Torkel suggested it. His mum already had a namesake in his first daughter, Donie. Marianna has three sons, and Donie has a boy and a girl, so the Quest Saxer bloodline will persist, if not the Quest name. Can't expect every man to be as willing as dear old Pips was to take his wife's name."

Pip started humming.

"Did I say something wrong?" Magda asked.

"I'm glad your family has some future. I don't think ours has."

"You have a niece."

"She's my cousin once removed, and she's just split with the bloke she was living with. She's thirty-something. No kids." She fell silent for a few minutes, then said, "It's my own fault. I could have had children. I could have tried, at least, but then, Lupin didn't either."

"If your cousin has some, they'll be of your blood."

"If. She's kicked her partner to the kerb, for excellent reasons, and by the time she gets around to trusting another bloke it'll probably be too late for children."

"That's what I thought," Magda reminded.

"Yes, but you don't look anything like the age you claim. Clarkia does." Pip put off melancholy and peered out the window at a high wall with autumn-tinted trees rising above it. "Oh look — is that the botanical gardens?"

Magda followed her gaze. "No, the Royal Botanical Gardens are in Sydney two-thousand. We're in Windhill, and those are the Fairy Gardens."

"They're an initiative of my family," Pandora called from the front seat. "A couple of years back we hired someone to make wooden statues of Mum and Dad when they were young. You might have a look at them if you have time."

Pip bounced in her seat. "I'd love to. Gardens are one of my *things*."

This trip to Sydney was offering all sorts of lovely dividends already. And to think she'd vacillated about coming!

CHAPTER FIVE. DIAMOND SPELLMAN

Pip had little time to ponder her pleasurable plans before Pandora turned the car up another street and stopped in front of a modest building with high double doors.

Diamond Spellman Studio.

"I'll leave you to it," Pandora said. "Give me a call if you need a lift back, but Jasper will probably organise something if you mention it to him."

"She's miffed," Magda remarked to Pip, gathering her shawl around her. "Give my love to Davey and the kids," she added in a slightly louder voice as she climbed out of the vehicle. "How many are there now?"

"Three, the same as usual," Pandora said wearily. "Helene and Niamh and Duffy."

"*Their* kids, I meant."

"Frankly, I might have lost count of Niamh's. It's the twin thing."

"My mother was a twin," Pip put in. "But I'm not."

"Don't look at me," Pandora said. "It's all Davey. He's a twin and —"

Pip frowned. She'd thought the propensity for twins carried down the female line — if it carried at all.

"Goodbye," Pandora said.

Pip got out of the van and Pandora drove off.

"*Really* miffed," Magda said with evident relish. "I shouldn't wind her up, but it's got to be a habit. She's so *much* like Peter P, but I've never yet got her cross enough to swear."

"Do you want to?"

"Well, *he* does, and I want to know if she's as creative as he is. Even after all these years his wife just says, *Language, Peter!* every so often."

"That's probably why Pandora doesn't."

"You could be right. And I can tell you now, she has *not* forgotten how many grandchildren she has."

Pip looked up at the façade of the studio. "I've never been here before," she said. "Is it new?"

"Not especially. They were here in the nineties. Used to do documentaries where the film crew were part of the show. Mis-takes, assorted balls-ups . . . you name it, they showed it. It was like reality TV before that was a thing, and they were a real crew, not a manufactured one, and if they squabbled it wasn't scripted."

"I think I remember that," Pip said. "Particularly the pre-senter. Jasper Diamond, right? He's tall and handsome with a lopsided face. There was a smaller chap with flashy dress sense . . . Rod, something."

"Rod Bowen. That's them. His wife, Tasmyn, is one of the partners."

Pip nodded noncommittally. That must be the female pre-senter. Jasper Diamond's sister? Cousin, maybe?

They entered a sunny foyer where a woman with curly wheat-coloured hair sat behind a desk. She was stitching what looked like a Victorian petticoat. She glanced up with a quick, enquiring smile which turned astonished as she took in their appearance.

"Magda Quest Saxer," Magda introduced herself. "This is Pippin Pearmain, here for a screen test for *Half-Life of the Lost.* Should have been arranged by someone from Arts in Tune."

"That's right." The woman, whose name-badge stated her name as *Aberdeen Diamond,* set aside her sewing and tapped at her computer. "Matt's come up to supervise." Her smile was wry now, suggesting her company didn't need supervision. "I'll ring through and see if they're ready for you."

At that point, a door opened on the mezzanine level above and a tall man leaned over the rail and called, "Is that our ten o'clock I hear, Ab?"

The woman answered in the affirmative. "Can you see yourself up?" she added, glancing at the petticoat.

Magda said they could.

"Not what you'd call over-formal," she said audibly as they climbed a spiral stair.

"No . . . but who's Matt?"

"He's one of the directors of Arts in Tune, the art and music company on Delphinium Island. The film's being shot on their sound stage, and I gather they're providing the music and maybe some lighting and such. Joint enterprise."

Pip had no time to answer, because they'd reached the mezzanine and Jasper Diamond was holding out his hand, first to Magda then to Pip.

Pip stared at him. He looked much the way she remembered him from the documentaries, but older. Late fifties, maybe, she speculated — possibly eight or ten years her junior. His dark hair had faded but he still had considerable charisma.

"Come on in," he said to them both, ushering them into an open-plan room set up with multiple light banks, several flats, odd furnishings, and a forest of camera equipment.

Two other men looked up as they entered. One, who had been tinkering with a lighting board which cycled through pink, ghostly blue, and sunshine-analogue light, did the double take Pip was beginning to recognise from people encountering her and Magda for the first time. The other, a tall slim man with shaggy brown hair, favoured them with a delightful smile. He had on a polo-shirt with the logo *Arts in Tune,* so he must be the representative from Delphinium Island.

Pip wished she'd finished watching the documentary on the island when it had been on television back in February. It hadn't seemed relevant then, so she'd watched a bit and switched it off in favour of writing in her bucket list.

Must have been a Diamond Spellman production. If I'd watched it properly, I might have learned something useful.

While Magda talked to Jasper Diamond, Pip moved over to survey the other two men. She homed in on the one who'd looked startled. "Yes, I'm real. Yes, I really am this small, this old, and this—"

He reddened and held up both hands. "Sorry, sorry."

"No need to be sorry. I was just getting in first." Pip beamed at him. "Let's start again. I'm Pippin Pearmain. Who are you?"

"Stew," he said.

"No thanks, I had breakfast."

The man looked even more uncomfortable. "I mean, I'm Steward Bellaire—cameraman—camera*person*."

"Cameraman's fine by me, since you are a man. And I'd better not annoy you. You might focus on my bad side," Pip said.

He gave her a fascinated once over. "I don't think you have one, Ms Pearmain. Or is that *Miss*? Or *Missus*?"

"Huh! And yes, *Miss*. I'm not a manuscript, married, *or* miserable."

Serves me right, I suppose, for pulling his chain.

The cameraman walked to one side, assessing her.

"Asymmetrical, with interesting structure," he clarified. His hand moved out as if to touch her chin or her shoulder to turn her into the light, but he visibly held back.

Pip sighed inwardly. *Another one who's been educated out of behaving naturally.*

She held still and let him look. It was part of the job to be assessed at length, judged suitable or not, and treated like merchandise. She didn't mind. That was what she was.

The other man, the one from Arts in Tune, waited until the cameraman had finished his observation and gone back to messing with the lights before he introduced himself.

"Matin Campania, Miss Pearmain. Welcome to our first venture into creative film."

"I haven't had the screen test yet," Pip said, wondering where she'd heard the name before.

She'd once been on holiday to Campania with her cousins and Big Nanna de Leon, but that wasn't it.

She started to hum, not the high mosquito buzz that had so annoyed Lupin, but a lower, more musical rendition of "Silk and Circumstance." She'd taken to humming that, because it took her mind to her ballet-to-be which had almost replaced her bucket list as her happy inner landscape.

Suddenly, she broke off as puzzle pieces locked together in her mind. Jane had told her the waltz had been recorded by a fiddler named Campania—Tamzin Campania.

Arts. Arts in Tune. Tunes. Why not?

She fixed her attention on the young man, who looked to be in his early thirties, and a quarter century younger than anyone else in the room. He was maybe the same age as Zach. Younger than Tane and Jules, but older than Jamie and Finn.

Beautiful.

Oops. Pip dragged her comparative thoughts into order. Assessing people was a habit, but she didn't want to be done for—what the heck was it called when a single woman liked to look at men and compare and contrast them? This one was worth looking at. Lovely, in fact. He smelled nice, too, if one liked green peas. Pip did.

"Do you know a fiddle player named Tamzin Campania?" she asked him.

If he was surprised, he didn't show it. He just nodded, smiling. "She's my wife."

"Oh, good!" Pip clapped her hands as the puzzle finished itself in triumph. "I want to get her album—*Magic Fiddle,* because it's got "Silk and Circumstance" on it. Such a lovely tune. Do you sell it on the island, or would it be better to get it on-line? And if I wanted to use an excerpt for a ballet—not necessarily your wife's cover, but the tune itself, how would the copyright be managed?"

"We'll be selling it at the festival, and also the new one— *Lullabies for Music*," he said. "As to copyright, the tune itself is public domain, but I wouldn't call Tamzin's version a *cover*. To the best of our knowledge hers is the first official recording of it. Lovely, isn't it?"

Pip said, honestly, "I've only heard *of* her version, from a friend."

"But you know the tune?"

"Yes, I knew it a long time ago, in the seventies. An actor I worked with used to play it to me in the green room. Not on a fiddle though—he had a lute." Not wanting to think of her long-lost friend right then, she rocked forward on her toes and added, "What festival?"

"That one." Campania gestured towards a pile of posters on a table. "Have a look if you like."

Pip took herself off to the table, picked up a poster and turned it to the light, which had settled into sunlit-day-mode.

It showed an aerial impression of an island, with dancers in wide skirts twirling to produce circles of colour.

Arts in Tune Presents —
The Autumn Festival
Dance in Tune — April 17 — April 27

The small print listed names Pip didn't know, and enticingly-titled workshops and displays, but she'd seen enough. She flounced over to Campania. "I thought I was testing for a film part?"

"You are," he said.

She stabbed her finger at the poster. "This is a dance festival. How can you film in the middle of a dance festival?"

He said, "We put on four major festivals a year, each

showcasing a particular aspect of the arts, to capitalise on our infrastructure."

"What?"

"A lot of festival venues have trouble with a lack of accommodation, long lines for loos and food and so on. We built a dedicated venue, and to avoid having it idle for fifty-one weeks of the year, we decided to have multiple festivals — four major ones and smaller, more intimate groups in between. Sometimes, others hire the venue, though we only let it go to broadly-based arts or creative gatherings.

"With regular festivals, we can afford to have enough accommodation, and we have regular suppliers who bring food vans or work in the big main kitchen. We also have a loyal band of craft people, who bring herbs, wool, papermaking, woodwork, costume . . . any and all of those things are available for festival-goers who want quality products or to try their hand at something new.

"As for this film, our soundstage will be set up, and filming will take place over the week with a few days at the end for retakes. It's an added attraction for anyone interested in film making, and of course, any actors or crew not involved in a particular scene will be able to enjoy the festival."

"That's *nuts!*" Pip said. "The very *idea* of providing something interesting for off-scene performers goes against the grain of bored and suffering assets and terrible coffee in the green room. You'll be *lynched* for resetting the bar too high for most companies to compete."

"So we've been told, but our motive is not to upset others . . .we want to treat artists the way they deserve. We will provide coffee upon request but I'm afraid we can't stretch to *terrible*. One of our guest caterers would exclaim *Gott im Himmel!* at that idea." Campania's smile widened. "She might even make it to *Gross Gott im Himmel!*" which will send her minions scuttling in all directions."

Pip narrowed her eyes, suspecting him of playing with her. "Why haven't I heard of any of this before? It sounds massive."

"There was a documentary showcasing us in summer, but we haven't been going long. Our inaugural festival was back in winter last year. This is our first autumn outing, and we can't wait!"

He sounded properly enthusiastic.

"It must be a *lot* of work," Pip ventured.

Campania said, "It is, but three things make it work for us. One is top class providers. Last year we invited people. These days *they* approach *us*. Two is autonomy. The providers, workshop leaders, and performers are responsible for their own areas. We provide venue, a master program, and facilities. It's up to them to make it work. For first-timers, we provide a mentor who will advise and encourage. Three is the motto — arts in tune. Anyone *not* in tune, and not prepared to make a true effort to *be* in tune, may leave."

Pip gaped at him. "But what about the punters who've paid for a workshop or whatever?"

"The program states that any part of the program not available for whatever reason will be replaced by a cover of equal value. For *Dancing Arts* we had fifty percent more applications than we could fit in. We allowed some — the ones who could accept the offer in good faith — to come anyway, as guests. They are available to help anyone the mentors think might be overwhelmed, and in the event of trouble they can and will provide the cover." His kindly face stiffened, and steel came into his voice as he said softly, "It's amazing how *hard* people will work to lift their game and adjust their attitude if they know the understudies are waiting and hoping."

"What if an understudy sabotages someone to steal the gig?" Pip asked.

"It's never happened. If it did, the guilty party would be

turned over to the wronged party for justice."

"Is that legal?"

"It's never been tested, but everyone involved — including guests — signs an agreement promising to behave in a manner that will not bring harm to anyone else."

Pip spotted the flaw in that. "Aha!" she exclaimed in triumph. "That means the wronged party, who has also signed the agreement, can't bring *harm* to the guilty party."

"Exactly. That means the guilty person must *undo* the harm. We've thought it out in depth. My wife's foster father is a solicitor, and he went over the agreement with a magnifying glass and drew it up officially. He worked his way through a dozen and a half tarts while he did it, so we know it was a thorough job."

Pip gazed at him in admiration. "That's *fiendish*."

"Thank you. My wife said so too. It even impressed her foster-brothers, and that's a rare occurrence." He flashed her a complicit smile, then cocked his head to one side.

"Speaking of impressive, I think my wife would like to paint you, if you don't object."

Pip, who had been painted five times in various roles but never as herself, thought that would be interesting. "Okay, if I have time," she said.

Campania looked a bit surprised, blinked, and visibly changed the subject. "Come over and I'll show you one of the scenes."

"I haven't seen any sides."

"Never mind." He turned to Jasper Diamond, who was still talking to Magda. "Jasper, have we got a Perdita yet?"

"Not in my pocket, no," Diamond said. "We've cast one, but she's not here." He glanced speculatively at Magda.

"Not on your bloomin' life, you pirate. Grab the blonde from downstairs."

CHAPTER SIX. SCREEN TEST

Jasper went out and hollered down from the mezzanine. Shortly thereafter, the woman, Aberdeen, who was presumably his wife, came up.

Jasper dragged an old couch away from the wall. "Feel like a nap, sweetheart?"

"I suppose that means you want me to have one." Aberdeen subsided onto the couch and closed her eyes. Evidently, she was used to odd requests.

"Okay, do your stuff," Jasper called.

Campania said, "This is a hospital room. Perdita has been lying in her coma for ten years. I'm her brother. You're—"

"Her consciousness. *I* know."

Pip sank cross-legged onto the floor and dropped her chin in her hands. She started to hum.

Campania mimed opening a door and stepped over to gaze at Aberdeen . . . or rather, at Perdita. He had a page of script in his hand.

"Perdie? Perdie?" He sighed and shook his head. "Ten years. They said you'd be awake in a few days, then a few weeks, then they just switched from *will be,* to *might be* and now it's *probably not.*" He paused, and the slightest tilt of his head suggested a cue.

Pip stopped humming and shook her head. Then she tilted it and smacked her ear. "That's better," she remarked. She turned to stare at Campania. "You were saying?"

She dropped out of character and glanced at Diamond. "What's his name? Her brother?"

"Oz," Diamond supplied.

Pip repeated the line, "You were saying? Come on, Oz, I haven't got all day. You were emoting away, but I couldn't hear you."

Campania bent and gazed at Perdita. "Wake up! We're all waiting, treading water!"

"That's your fault," Pip said. She put her hands on the floor, untangled her legs and rose into a downward dog before getting to her feet and stretching. She danced a few steps, miming treading water. Then she floated towards Perdita's brother and said, "Boo!"

He didn't react.

Pip crossed her arms. "Dammit, Oz. You're no fun. That always used to make you squeal like a little girl."

Campania wandered to the foot of the couch and pretended to pick up something, possibly a medical chart. "Vital signs, good—why won't you just wake up!" He dropped the chart and left the room in a hurry.

Pip slid back into her cross-legged position. "I don't know. I just—don't know." She plopped her chin back into her hands.

"Cut!"

Pip jumped and looked up. Campania was back, extending a hand to help her up, but she was on her feet before he got there.

"Get anything?" Diamond asked the cameraman.

Steward Bellaire did a double thumbs-up. "She's a lively one."

"*She's* the cat's mother," Pip observed.

Diamond put his hand up, maybe to hide a grin. "Okay— now the scene where Oz and Stevo—the husband—fight over pulling the plug. Have we got a Stevo?"

"Don't look at me," Steward said, hoisting the camera.

Jasper Diamond went out to the mezzanine a second time

and hollered, "Rod!"

A smaller and rather dapper man came in. "What now?"

"You. Stevo. The husband. Your wife's been in a coma for twenty-five years."

"God, has she?" He looked alarmed.

Proper comedians the lot of them!

Pip shook her head, but realised they were probably inhabiting long-accustomed roles. Jasper Diamond was playing *the boss,* and this one must be the comic relief.

Diamond handed Rod a page of script and gave another one to Campania.

He gestured to the cameraman. "Okay?"

Up went the thumb. "Hit me!"

The two men read the dialogue and moved as the script directed. They were natural, but Pip had no sense of performance. They were placeholders.

She perched on a visitor's chair and looked from one to another like a spectator at a tennis match as they ding-donged back and forth. Oz, the brother, wanted to keep his sister alive, while Stevo, the husband, tried to point out his position as a man married in name only, with no chance to build a family.

"Divorce her, then!"

"But she's done nothing wrong!"

"No fault. According to . . ." Oz reeled off a lot of legalese.

"Studied up on it, have you? Want to get rid of me?"

As the argument grew more bitter, Pip frowned, put her hands over her ears, then started to rock.

After a last spurt of anger, the men stormed out, with nothing resolved. Pip stopped rocking and took her hands away, looking from side to side. Then she got up and tiptoed over to the oblivious Perdita.

"That didn't sound good. They might be going to end us. Maybe that would be best." She walked over to an imaginary bank of instruments and pretended to hold an electrical plug.

"Shall I save them the trouble?" Then she shrugged and moved back to the bed, where she lay down on the floor in the same pose as Perdita.

She would have joined her on the couch if there had been room.

"Cut."

The other men returned, and the cameraman conferred with Diamond. Aberdeen sat up. "Can I go back to my sewing?"

"Thanks, sweetheart."

Aberdeen got off the couch. "Want a cup of tea?" she asked Pip.

"That depends. Do you have herbal tea?"

"You bet. Mum's a mad keen gardener and Jasper's nearly as bad. Come on to the kitchen and see what we've got."

"Hang on—" Stew waved vigorously. "I need some light shots."

"I'll have the tea ready," Aberdeen mouthed, and left the room.

Pip moved into the spotlight and stood patiently while Stew circled her, stopping now and again to adjust the lighting or change lenses or cameras.

"Try some moves," he said.

Pip bent, stretched, slumped, rolled into a ball, jumped and threw in some shadowboxing, fencing moves and ballet.

She waited for a change of clothing or makeup shots, but Stew asked her to tie up her hair with light shining on her face. He nodded to someone to throw her a soccer ball to bounce and catch and asked her to open an umbrella.

"Scream."

Pip gave a soundless scream, then another one at full volume, channelling Banshee Mary in the whistle register she'd developed long ago with Sully.

It went on.

"Can you jump into someone's arms?"

"Yes, as long as he guarantees to catch me," Pip said.

"I want to try . . ." Stew went off into a huddle with Diamond and they rigged up a sheet between the camera and the light.

"Matin—"

Campania nodded assent. "I can catch her." He held out his arms to show the way and Pip flashed back to being held in the same fashion while Tane jumped into the sea.

At least there's no cold water this time.

"Count me down," she said.

Diamond counted as Jane had, and on three, Pip started a run. She jumped, bringing her knees up, and Campania caught her deftly, lifted her above his head, which suggested he was at least as strong as Tane, turned, then deposited her gently on the floor.

"You're a dancer?" she asked.

He shook his head. "I *can* dance—Tamzin and I go to balls and ceilidhs sometimes—but I don't know any ballet, if that's what you mean."

Stew pulled the sheet down and tossed it aside. "Thanks for that, Miss Pearmain. I don't know that you'll be called to go in for calisthenics, but I wanted some action shots. Perdita is still, and we want contrast in her avatar."

Pip nodded. This worked with her own notion of stylised moves to make while the visitors to the hospital room looked straight through her.

"You seem fit."

Since he didn't add *for your age,* Pip said amiably that she enjoyed ballet, gardening, and beachcombing and had lately been swimming and riding.

Let him think I've been training up for the role.

He smiled and said he'd look forward to working with her. This seemed a bit premature to Pip, but she smiled back and shook his hand.

Having been released, she went downstairs and followed the kitchen sounds to a room where she drank tea with Aberdeen Diamond and someone who said she was Tasmyn Bowen. A younger woman with very fair hair came in, rattled things in the fridge, then went out again with a nod.

"That was Allirra," Aberdeen said.

Since she had curls like Aberdeen and eyes the same colour as Jasper's, Pip surmised she must be their daughter.

Pip drank her tea, which was a mixture of sage and marigold, and listened to the other women conversing with the ease of old friends.

"Which of you are going to the festival?" she asked in a gap in the conversation.

"Stew and Jasper, probably, and a couple of other camera people. The rest of us might drop in from time to time," Tasmyn said.

Aberdeen put in, "I've been looking at the costume briefs, but it's mostly street wear, vintage sixties coming up to modern. Perdita's going to be in a series of simple nightdresses, probably cream or ivory to match with the wedding dress idea, and I think you wear the things she would depending on what year it is . . . if that makes sense?"

"It does, but can we use a few . . ." Pip got up and did a toy soldier march, then an Irish jig.

"Yes! There's a sequence at the beginning where you're trying to get the family to notice you. Later, you realise they don't and can't, so you get more outrageous and finally — "

Pip broke in, "I haven't seen the script. Do I need to strip?"

Aberdeen looked nonplussed.

"Wouldn't be the first time. It would work on the consciousness-stripped-bare idea."

Tasmyn gave her a slow smile. "I can see why Humphrey wanted *you*, Miss Pearmain."

Who's Humphrey?

Pip persisted, "Does she wake up, or not?"

"She . . . yes, she does, but only after the decision is made to switch off on the sixtieth anniversary when almost everyone has stopped visiting. Then it's up to interpretation as to whether she *is* awake and may be able to function or if she's dying."

"What happens to me?"

"That's also open to interpretation. You finally leave the room, but whether you run out joyfully or creep out, losing substance as you go . . ."

Pip ran through the sequences in her mind. "I'll be scared. After spending sixty years wanting *out*, I'll be heading into the unknown, and believing it might be oblivion." She snapped her fingers and let herself collapse like a marionette with cut strings. "Maybe I melt back into her. That would be difficult onstage, but you could do an effect in post-production."

Then she got up and resumed sipping her tea. "That's if I get cast. Who has the say, anyhow?"

"The playwright, oddly enough," Aberdeen said.

"Who's that?"

"His name is Humphrey Carpenter-Rivers. He's one of those people who float around the fringes of the arts. He submitted this script when we were looking for a joint project with Arts in Tune. It was a bit of a rush job, but evidently he wrote it back in the nineties, and fished it out when he read the brief. It's not something the mainstream would invest in."

"He's not here, though?" Pip looked through the kitchen, half expecting a gentleman to pop out of the under-kettle cupboard. She *liked* the Diamond Spellman studio. They had proper tea. She'd never drunk sage-and-marigold before, but she understood the combination was good for memory, circulation, and skin afflictions. She didn't have any problems with those, but people her age often did, so she quite saw where Aberdeen was coming from.

Tasmyn said, "Humph'll have a look at the screen test, but he's not likely to say no, because he wrote the part with you in mind originally."

Pip felt her eyebrows shoot up.

"So he said. He was lamenting that he hadn't got it to fly in the nineties when you were still working."

"I *am* still working," Pip objected. She considered explaining how Little Mum and Sully had gone to glory in the same week, leaving her without an agent or immediate family. The Sullivan Gilbert Agency had continued, but without Sully at the helm it limped along and stalled until Magda gave it a good shake-up. Whatever they'd done in the failing years hadn't involved getting any roles, or even potential roles, for tiny Pippin Pearmain.

She decided not to bother with the explanation. Let them think she'd been in plays and things they hadn't seen.

"So we discovered, when Humph got the bit between his teeth and bearded Missus Saxer in her lair," Tasmyn said.

"Not literally," Aberdeen put in. "But evidently the staff had *lost* you, so to speak. Missus Saxer muttered something about delegation being crap and —"

"Found me," Pip supplied. "I never actually retired, so here I am."

"And you've barely changed," Aberdeen said warmly.

"Fossilised," Pip agreed.

"No — you do look older than in most of your films, but you look like *you*."

Pip nodded. She'd often thought she became more herself as she aged. Maybe that was because she'd never had a family to diffuse her attention from doing more or less as she pleased.

"Humph said he didn't want to meet you at present, because it would spoil the mystique," Tasmyn said. Her expression showed what she felt of that, and Pip concurred.

"I don't have mystique. I just do what's wanted."

"Not method acting?"

"I don't think there's an official term for what I do. I just do it."

"Once Humph has cast an eye over the rushes . . . well, the test . . . I reckon you'll be *just doing* a lot more," Tasmyn opined.

"You didn't see the test."

"Aberdeen did."

Considering Aberdeen had been lying on the couch pretending to be in a coma, Pip didn't think she could have seen much, but maybe she'd had her eyes open some of the time.

"*Creepy-ethereal* was what she said," Tasmyn added.

"Good. That's what I was going for."

Pip had never bothered much about the business side. Sully used to take care of it. She supposed Magda would do the same, but she asked, "Who, exactly, is hiring me? If I get hired? And I assume I get paid?" She knew ten years was a long time in the entertainment industry.

Aberdeen said, "It's a joint enterprise between us and Arts in Tune, and there are grants and some crowd-funding in place. You'll be paid as an actor, and also as a provider for the festival, if that makes sense. The festival payment is flexible because they work as a collective, covering expenses, then paying out a percentage."

"Good. Sully always said doing things for nothing got you nothing."

"Sully?"

"My agent before Magda. Her name was Sullivan Gilbert."

Again, she felt it too complicated to explain how Sully had gone to glory and how Magda had appointed herself just a few days earlier.

Fortunately, Magda and the men came in at that point and joined them for tea, coffee and, to Pip's pleasure, some tarts that were unmistakably from the *Queen of Tarts* bakery.

She pounced on a Strawberry Fool on the Hill. "Yum! I have a standing order for these at Jelly-and-Juice." She saw the others didn't understand, so she added, "That's my local café. In Tasmania."

Aberdeen said, "Ours come direct from Fiddle Bay where they're produced. We have a regular delivery." She added, "So, you flew up . . .when?"

"Wednesday evening," Pip said. She added, reflectively, "The plane people don't know how to make proper tea."

PART TWO. THE FAIRY GARDENS

April 2022

CHAPTER ONE. FAIRY GARDENS

After leaving Diamond Spellman, with the promise of news as soon as Humphrey Carpenter-Rivers had given his opinion, Magda suggested a walk to the Fairy Gardens.

"I'll leave you to look round, while I go and hunt up Panda and ask for a lift," she said.

Considering Magda had refused Jasper Diamond's offer of transport back to the guesthouse, Pip considered that peculiar, but she didn't comment.

"I'm actually going to make my peace with her, if I can," Magda added, sighing. "The older I get, the less empathy I seem to have. Poor kid."

"Have you known her long?" Pip asked. She discounted Magda's description of Pandora as a *kid*, knowing the woman was older than she looked. She supposed most people struck Magda that way.

"I've known her since the seventies when she walked into *Magdala Gallery*. Remember? I told you I recognised whose child she must be. Until then she had no idea she wasn't Jacobi's daughter, or even of the same order. Since I'd been in a roughly similar situation in regards to Mum and Francine, I had some fellow feeling with her."

Pip frowned at her. "Order?"

Magda said impatiently, "You must know some of the orders. You were grilling Edgar about them earlier."

"The encyclopaedia he said he'd lend me, you mean."

"It's called *Orders of the Fay*, and it's one of those unclassifiable productions. Not quite an encyclopaedia, not a coffee

51

table book, not anecdotes . . . a compendium, perhaps. There's a new edition illustrated by Pen Inkersoll — the Magic Cat artist — who happens to be Panda's daughter-in-law. I don't know if that's the edition Edgar and Joan have, but it's definitely the one to buy if you're looking to own it."

"I probably will end up buying it."

"So?" Magda looked from side to side and chose a street to the left. "Hope this is the way."

"So — what?"

"Obviously, someone has disclosed to you at some point. What's *your* experience with the fay? What do you know, when did you find out and how pervasive is the knowledge in your life?"

Pip said, cautiously, "I *think* it may have begun when I was little. Little Mum had a book called *Grandmother's Sunshine* . . . It belonged to one of her ancestors and was handed down through the family." By the time she'd explained what she knew and something of her recent V-S Experience on *Tulpenmanie* and *over there,* they'd reached the Fairy Gardens.

Magda indicated the narrow gates. "These will be the statues Panda mentioned. Crikey!"

Pip looked up, and her heart jolted. The super-life-size statues showed a man and a woman stepping forward from their plinths, holding hands to form an arch for anyone entering. They were carved from an unfamiliar wood, unpainted, but glowing with life and vigour.

"Panda's mum, Barbie Hanover as-was, and Jacobi le Fay," Magda said, looking up. "Impressive, aren't they? I've never been too sure of Barbie. She's charming and gracious, but I've always felt it was a mask — a façade — for the real person underneath. Seeing this representation of her makes me think maybe Jacobi was more than just a convenient stand-in father for Panda. Having a visible father *mattered* in those days."

Pip put her hand on the plinth to her left. "I *love* this wood.

Who made them? Panda said the family hired someone, but she didn't say who."

Magda shrugged. "Don't know. This is the first time I've seen them. There might be a signature somewhere, or we can ask Panda."

Pip found a signature etched in a brass plate, covered with what might have been Perspex, screwed into the plinth low down to the side. It showed a photo of the couple and also some biographical details, but she ignored those in favour of scanning for the artist.

Carved by Xavier Partridge of Marmalade Woodcraft.

"I've *got* to find him," Pip said.

"Why? To go all fan-girl?"

"I never go fan-girl. I have to find him because he's going to make me a bucket. By the way, do you do decoupage?"

Magda gave her a hard stare. "Do I look like someone who does decoupage Miss Pearmain?"

"How should I know? My parents and grandparents were all good at different crafts, but none of them did decoupage. I wonder if it's something one can learn from a book."

"I daresay. What do you want to decorate?"

"A bucket," Pip said. She'd thought that was clear already.

"You want this Xavier Partridge to make you a beautifully carved bucket so you can glue Victorian scrap on it?"

"No, that would be a waste. I want him to make me *a* bucket. I'm going to glue things on a different bucket."

"I see." Magda gave her a funny look.

Then she went off to find and to mollify Pandora, and Pip, pleased to be alone for a while, entered the Fairy Gardens.

For an hour she rambled along winding paths, gazed out over the sea from a tiny cliff, dabbled her hands in miniature waterfalls and rubbed the leaves in the scented garden between her finger and thumb. She found a natural stage that reminded her of the chalk ground where she'd danced with Jane and the sward near the castle. She spent some time there blocking out more of her dolphin ballet. Her mind buzzed with possibility.

Matin Campania was her conduit for getting hold of some dolphin music. She wanted to interview his wife, too, in the hope of identifying more public domain tunes. She thought *educational use* might be presented as a reason for what was called *fair usage,* but what if she didn't end up being able to work with the school at Jellico Bay? It would be better to find music she could use free and clear.

She determined she'd go to the festival, even if she didn't get the film part. The cats and Clarkia knew she might be away for ten days or so, and she'd make the most of it. There was the book Edgar was going to lend, and . . . She stopped planning as it struck her she hadn't considered the soloist— or principal dancer—for her ballet. There had to be one—the human point-of-view character. Even if the dolphins were danced by children, the soloist would need to be trained for pointe work.

Not me.

Pip knew she wasn't good enough for what she had in mind. Enthusiasm, good health, flexibility, and experience could take her only so far, and at her age, she couldn't hope for dramatic improvement in her technique.

What was needed was true talent and inspiration, that in-born spark that lit up craft and technique from within.

Jane?

Jane would *look* perfect, with her slightly foreign features and graceful physique. She was—what? A quarter waterfolk, a quarter pisky, part human and the rest was sylvan. She was beautiful, dedicated and determined, but she wasn't good enough—yet. At seventeen or so she'd come late to ballet, but she had plenty of time to hone her skills. Jamie's sister was teaching her. Was Laura a professional teacher, or just some-one like Pip who knew some ballet?

Pip sighed. She needed someone seriously good, with serious experience and the spark that lit her up from inside. Or him. Her soloist could be a man.

Or would someone that good make unskilled children look too amateurish in contrast?

And what about the shark? Or was it going to be a squid?

Ought to get that seafay man . . . Lore . . . something.

No, he'd terrify kids, and I doubt if he ever comes through the gates. He'd probably be arrested on sight.

She considered the transformation where the dolphins danced as other beings.

Cats. Pip hugged herself. *Amberjill!*

She pictured the back-up cat in her games with blowing leaves, twigs and, on one startling occasion, a well-clawed lemon. The twists and leaps were a variation on the dolphins' steps.

She hadn't got music for that, yet, but it would be joyful, and it *had* to be a fiddle, and maybe a flute.

Oh.

She sketched in the dance moves . . . might she call it *catrobatics,* or was that too twee? A big ball of wool, maybe, might make some comedy and —

Oh again!

She *could* be in her ballet. She was no soaring soloist, but she could absolutely play an old queen cat who still had it! She'd dance and get tangled in the wool, and maybe fall over and the other cats would support her because she was family and they loved her.

I can get Kittisack and Amberjill to show me some moves.

The natural stage in the Fairy Gardens was perfect because she was able to judge distances by orienting on various natural features. It was exactly the right size for staging an outdoor ballet, though that might rule out pointe work.

She was still gleefully plotting moves and scenes when her phone rang in her messenger bag.

She scrabbled for it. "Magda?"

"Where are you?" Her agent sounded curious rather than miffed.

Pip looked left and right, seeking landmarks. "Still in the gardens. Near a kind of chapel."

"I don't know the garden layout, so if I come to look for you we'll keep missing one another. Can you get yourself back to the gates?"

"Yes, of course," Pip said with more hope than expectation. Her sense of direction had never been very good. She glanced around her impromptu stage, read a few artfully placed signs which might have sent her to *the sandstone outcrop*, to *the fernery*, or to *the rose arbour* and chose what she hoped was the right path.

She walked for ten minutes before realising it wasn't.

She might have wandered for another hour had she not seen a wooden sign indicating *Founders' Gate*.

That reminded her of her bucket-related ambitions, and as she strode to meet Magda, she wrestled her phone into *find-me* mode and ran a search for *Xavier Partridge Marmalade Woodcraft*.

A number popped up and Pip, never one to wait unnecessarily, unless she had chosen to procrastinate, hit *call*.

The mobile you have called . . . click! Transferring you now.

She heard a ring tone and, after a few cracks and popples, someone said, "Hello?"

It was a woman's voice, so probably *not* Xavier Partridge, Pip thought, although one never knew these days.

"I'd like to speak to Xavier Partridge," Pip said. "The sculptor. Is this his—I mean the right phone?"

"Yes, but he's not here. He'll be back next month."

"Back from where?"

"Sailing."

A clatter made Pip jerk the phone away from her ear.

"Sorry. I dropped it. Could be worse. I dropped a phone in

the custard once."

"Did it survive?"

"I stuck it in dry rice . . . do you know that trick? Anyway, I got a husband out of the situation, so it was totally worth it. I'm Frances le Fay. I'll take a message for Xav if you explain what you want him for."

Le Fay . . .

Synchronicity jangled in Pip's ears. "Um, are you any relation to Jacobi le Fay? The Fairy Gardens man? I'm at the gardens now."

"I'm not related to him, but my husband's connected somehow or other. Don't ask me how, exactly. Niall's got dozens of cousins, including one who's the professor who married *my* cousin and Xav, who's a sculptor, as you know. Then there's one who makes sweets and runs a cafe—Flick, her name is. She's an angel. But that's—"

A baby wailed in the background, reminding Pip of little Tallien. Another joined in.

"Dammit, the twins! Ought to have named them Call and Echo instead of Seraphina and Francisco. Serra and Cisco, usually, since I hate being called Fran and wouldn't wish it on my son. Vange!" she called out suddenly. "Nappy time!"

"Is Vange your nanny?" Pip asked, hoping someone would take charge of the babies so she could get Frances back to the subjects of Xavier Partridge and the bucket.

"No, Vange is our eldest. Evangeline. Big help. Dammit, I'm leaking milk again . . . quick, what do you want with Xav?"

"I want him to carve me a bucket," Pip said.

"Ooh, wonderful! He'll do that, I'm sure. What's your name?"

"Pippin Pearmain." Pip considered her email address, but that was easy to get wrong, so she gave her number instead.

"Got it! One bucket for Pippin Pearmain. I'll get Xav to call you as soon as he and Nel get off the galleon. Can't catch them now because they'll still be out of service."

"Thanks," Pip said. She added, "When are they likely to be off the galleon?"

"I don't know, but it shouldn't be too much longer. Tell you what, drop by for lunch or supper sometime," Frances said. "It's a mad house here at present, but we could always convene at the Dark Room. In fact . . . yes, we'll do that. Flick and Chas's George is brilliant with the kids. If Ran's there so much the better . . . They can take my lot and Joyful to the playground so we can hear ourselves think."

The background wail intensified.

"Toodles," Frances said, and hung up.

Pip had nearly reached the gate, where Magda leaned, apparently chatting with the statues.

"Toodles," Pip said to Magda with belated indignation. "She said toodles and hung up on me. Who does that?"

Chapter Two. Orders of the Fay

"I don't know," Magda said, straightening. "Who does say that?"

"She also asked me to lunch or to supper at a café, where someone called George will wrangle her twins."

"Who is *she*?" Magda enquired.

"Frances le Fay, she said."

"Why did she ring you? Does she know you?"

"She didn't ring me. I rang her. That is, I rang Xavier Partridge, the Marmalade Woodcraft man, about my bucket. I got her instead. Apparently he's on a galleon, if that makes sense. It doesn't to me. Who goes on a galleon?"

"The Marmalade Woodcraft man, evidently," Magda said dryly. "It does make sense to me, and I think that brings us round full circle. I know you had that little book from your mother, but who disclosed to you regarding *over there* and the fay?"

"I suppose that would be Tane," Pip said, after some thought, although Tane hadn't explained much. Seeing Magda didn't know the name, she continued, "If you remember, Cousin Lupin left a V-S voucher for me, and I spent it on an Experience. Tane was the one who jumped into Bass Strait with me."

Magda nodded in comprehension. "That's right."

"How did *you* get disclosed to?" Pip asked.

Magda said, "I've always known. Remember I said I got in boarders partly because I needed someone who had the same knack as Mum?"

"Yes."

"Mum had enough alpenfee blood to open the gateways to *over there.* Because she was actually my grandmother, and my grandfather — whoever he was — was human, that made me a trace fay which means what you think it does. I'm like those people who do okay at school . . . maybe third in a class of twenty . . . *great work, Magda!* but when you put them in a class of a two hundred they're thirtieth which is the same in theory, but which looks like nothing much."

"It *is* the same though," Pip argued.

"Exactly the same, proportionately speaking, but look at it this way. If twenty runners take part in a race, who gets the bronze medal?"

"The one who comes third," Pip said.

"Right. If two hundred runners take part, who gets the bronze medal?"

"The one who comes third — oh, I see. The one who comes thirtieth wouldn't rate a mention."

"*Now* you see. I have better health than straight humans, and I've lived a good while longer than anyone expected, which makes me wonder about the disappeared Francine's pedigree. Mum said she was a quarterling alp maid, but I suspect there was a bit of sylvan in the mix. If so, it's just about possible she's still alive out there."

"Are you going to look for her?"

"I am not. She left me and never came back. Whatever she was, or is, the human genes trump the fay in me in every area other than lifespan. I can *see* the gateways, more or less, like shadows swimming in the mist, but I can't open them. I can't even touch them. My fingers go straight through. It's as frustrating as having permission to go into a beautiful garden but finding the gates locked and spikes along the wall. It's like seeing the coin you dropped behind the fridge just peeping around the corner and a finger-length out of reach.

"When Mum went, her fay talent went with her. That left me unable to go *over there* unless I could get someone to escort me. That someone turned out to be Peter P, bless him."

Pandora's natural father.

"He's not human?"

"Not in the least. He's a pixie man. Barbie le Fay is human, so that makes Panda a straight pixie-human halfling. That's another reason she rejects the idea of Peter P as her dad. Jacobi's an elf man, so Panda's brother Jakin and sister Carolyn are elf halflings."

"Why does that matter?"

"It doesn't. Well, not to anyone but Panda. And she's not even a purist. Her husband, Davey, is a fine old mash-up. I can't say exactly what's biting her . . . maybe just because she doesn't match her siblings. Maybe because Carolyn was one of those enchanting blonde children everyone loves while Panda was dark and — well, you've seen her. She's a wee bit astringent. Peter P says that's down to his grandfather Alexis Peckerdale who was, in his words, *a cranky old git.* But if you ask me, whatever it is, it's past time she got over it."

She stared into space for a bit. "Where was I? Right. I lost Mum *and* my access to *over there* at the same time. Peter P suggested fay boarders, who could let me through. I had one for a few weeks and it worked a treat, but she needed to move on, so I got Donie. Tork came as an unexpected part of the package. The Saxers are pure alpenfee, and my Marianna is half-and-a-bit, so I got my access privileges back and a dear life companion and two fine daughters into the bargain." She ruffled up her white hair, pressing her braid into place. "Using the gates sure beats flying. If I want to call on Peter P and Pia, *which* I do quite often, I get Tork or one of our girls to let me through the Tom Cat Hill gate, grab an escort — tree maids and hob men are always helpful — and in twenty minutes or so I'm passing through the pixie forest gate to annoy Peter P and get all the gossip from Pia."

Pip nodded doubtfully. Before she could enquire further, Pandora arrived in her van.

She smiled at Pip. "What did you think of my parents as rendered in wood?" She put the slightest emphasis on *parents* and gave Magda a sideways flick of a glance.

"I think they're beautiful," Pip said honestly. "I've decided the sculptor is going to make me a bucket."

Pandora glanced at Magda again, this time in baffled enquiry.

"Do you know Frances le Fay?" Pip continued.

Pandora's face took on a mildly terrified look.

"I see you do," Pip said.

"She's married a kind of distant cousin of Dad's," Pandora said, sounding as if it wasn't distant enough for her taste. "She's madly hospitable, madly enthusiastic, madly gorgeous and madly . . . mad. She collects friends, whether they like it or not. She loves everyone. She got married in a sheet. She's — unclassifiable."

"So I gathered," Pip said.

"And, as you have no le Fay blood whatsoever, her children are *not* related to you," Magda said bracingly.

Pandora glared at her. "Do you *want* to walk back to the guesthouse, Mistress Saxer?" Then she shrugged, and said, "On the other hand, as you pointed out, I don't have to call cousin with the glorious Frances. On the other, other hand, I *am* landed with Corin and . . . what's his name? That green one who tosses pixie dust at people. The scary one with the scarier sister."

"Peckerdale and Promise Grene," Magda supplied. "And that's *no* way to refer to your nephews and niece."

"And bloody Jisinia — Lord save me from bloody Jisinia!"

"Would that be the same Jisinia who has two-coloured eyes, an internal cat, and a pet human named Zach?" Pip asked. "She made my phone jump into her hand. I don't know *how* she did it, but she did. Only Zach made her give it back. That was before Tane trod on me, fed me figs then jumped overboard. That Jisinia?"

"Bloody damme to *hell!*" Pandora said forcefully, and Magda laughed.

When Pandora left them at the terrace house, Pip sought out Edgar. She found him in the kitchen up to his elbows in a giant bowl of dough.

"You'll be wanting t' books, lass," he said in his comfortable growl.

Pip smiled. He was direct. She liked direct.

"There." Edgar used his elbow to point over to the kitchen table.

As Pip approached, she saw that what she'd taken for a large book was really a slip-case containing a set of seven volumes.

"Take them upstairs and have a good look," Edgar said. "I'll bring you a cup of tea when I get t' dough worked up."

Pip thanked him. She gathered the slip-case into her arms, bore it up the stairs and laid it on her bed.

It was beautiful. The slip-case was patterned in green and gold, showing an intricate dance of characters interspersed with trees and waterfalls.

"Ahhh."

Here was the world of *Grandmother's Sunshine* – the world of the castle, the fossmere and the village of *Smile o' the Glean.*

Pip slipped out the first volume. *Alpenfee, Braefolk and Courtfolk,* by Piers le Fay. It was also figured in green and gold.

She opened the cover with gentle care and read the inscription.

With the author's gratitude for insights imparted by the Treadwell den.

Den . . . How odd. Magda had also mentioned that. Did some hobs live in dens, then, like wombats and foxes?

Setting that notion aside, Pip turned to the preamble, then paged on to what really interested her.

Alpenfolk.

That was Magda's order, in so far as she had one.

Pip learned that the alpenfolk, or alpenfee, occasionally styled alpmaids and alpmen, were fay who were associated with, or possibly descended from, humans from the Alpine regions of Switzerland, Austria and parts of Germany. The men were *tals* and the women *mädchens* if one wanted to be formal. Theirs was one of the orders who found it comfortable in the human realm, because they could all *pass.*

Pass as *what*? Human?

Many, but by no means all, were tall, robust people with fair or brown hair. They often had blue or grey eyes and tended to like Germanic names for their children.

Pip read on, absorbing information surrounding their order profile or personality, although the author cautioned against assuming they all conformed. She picked up tips on their clothing and their preferred diet and style, some of their dialect, their preferences, habits and some differences between alpenfee who lived in the alplands district *over there* and those who had *lived human* for generations.

The illustrations and diagrams helped to bring the people to life, and Pip pored over the pages until she almost expected to look up and find an alpland village of chalets with a tal in *lederhosen* playing an alphorn to a mädchen wearing a dirndl and plaiting her hair in a milkmaid braid.

"Magda Saxer," she said aloud. Her agent might be a trace fay, but her name and appearance conformed to the image in her mind. She ran through the other names Magda had dropped . . . two Mariannas, Torkel, Wilhelm and Idonea. Then there was her step-grandfather, Philip Quest, who had changed his name from *what*? Probably, he'd been human.

Pip was still playing with the connotations of what she'd read when someone tapped on her door.

"Yes? Come in," she called, expecting her tea.

"About time, too," Magda grumbled, surging into the room. She jerked her thumb behind her. "There's tea just there, stone cold. Edgar said he'd tapped on the door a few times but all the answer he got was a demented mosquito noise."

Pip looked at the tray. "I was reading. I'll drink it cold. Do you play the flugelhorn, Magda?"

Magda stared at her with hauteur. "I do not."

"Why not? You're alpenfee."

"I'm *trace* alpenfee. I'm mostly human."

"So? Humans play flugelhorns."

"*I* don't." Her face creased into a grin. "Torkel does, however. Mind you, so does Donie. They both play in a quartet called *Alpenstrudel* and yes, it's as cheesy as it sounds. Donie's party trick is playing a solo with an apple on her head. And *yes*, her man, whose name is Willi Teller — *does* shoot that apple off her head. At least, he pretends to. It's more conjuring than shooting."

Pip sighed contentedly as her attention wandered to the book. Magda's family sounded interesting, but the set of books represented a golden lode. She looked forward to hours of happy information-mining. She might not have time during her guesthouse stay to exhaust the possibilities of the fat collection, but she determined she was going to own a set of these books. In fact — she picked up her phone.

"Now what are you up to?" Magda asked, seating herself in the armchair near the bed.

Pip raised a finger for silence and hit a number she had on speed dial.

"Jonquil? This is Pippin Pearmain. I want books."

Chapter Three. Prevaricating with Jonquil

Jonquil Orange's voice said, "Straight to the point, as usual, I see Pip. What books do you want this time?"

"There's a series called The Orders of the Fay, by Piers le Fay. And I want the deluxe edition in the slip-case. Do you have it in stock?"

"We always try to have a couple of sets of that one in stock. It's under the radar, but we get a lot of repeat sales, with the second set going for housewarming or birthdays—or what some people call betrothal gifts."

"Better send me two then. Or three. I want my cousin and her daughter to have one. Do you still have my address on file?"

"We do. I can reel it off by heart. Lemonwood Cottage, six Ribston Lane, Jellico Bay."

"That's it. Do I get a discount for three sets?"

"No, but you'll save on postage, and you *do* get your members' discount."

"Excellent. Is there any book you *can't* get?"

"Obviously there are some. We do our best though. Is there one in particular you're after?"

"I was wondering if you have copies of a children's book called *Grandmother's Sunshine*."

She held her breath.

"No."

"Oh. Can you get it in?"

"No."

Pip was surprised at Jonquil's uncompromising tone. "Never heard of it?"

"Hmmm. I wouldn't say that."

"Hmmm? What does that mean?"

"It means, Hmmm. I have and I haven't."

Pip started to hum. It was unlike Jonquil to be cryptic. They'd never met, and Pip didn't know where the physical Orange Grove book shop was . . . or even if there *was* a physical one. She'd dealt with the Oranges for several years, but always by telephone, mail or email. They used to have a shop called Oranges and Lemons in Adelaide, but when they'd moved on, *flitted*, in fact, they'd sent her a heads-up. There had been an important omission in their message. They'd given her a new phone number, but no new address.

Over the years she'd dealt with them, wherever they were, they'd almost always had, or acquired, the books she wanted.

Jonquil said, "Are you there, Pippin? There's a buzz on the line."

"That was me. What do you mean by you have and you haven't—"

Tiny Pippin Pearmain had always been persistent, and she saw no reason to break the habit of six decades now.

"It means I *have* sort of heard of it. It's one of those elusive and possibly apocryphal treasures that collectors ask for and which booksellers with mottos like ours dread."

"There is a certain hubris in saying *If we haven't got it, we can get it, and if we can't get it, we'll orange well write it ourselves*," Pip said.

Jonquil sighed. "That's my husband's doing. I *told* him not to do that, but he *would*! Hubris is his second name. Anyway, there are other books of the same rarity and almost mythical status. One called *Granny Jean* caused quite a bit of excitement back in the days when magazines ran *book wanted* ads. I suspect one person advertised for it in error and others jumped on the bandwagon. I mean, if it's in print, it must be true . . . right?"

"Did anyone ever get one?" Pip asked.

"No, because it was a myth. Not a scam or fraud, because I doubt if the original advertiser meant any harm."

"How could anyone advertise for a book in error?"

"It was supposedly a final novel in the *Heather Jean* series, by the Scottish author Morag Bannock, but I believe someone conflated that idea with a real book with a different series heroine . . . Jenny Heatherdale from the *Call of the Glen* series. The author was Chanter Reed which is almost certainly a pen-name. That series *does* have a title called *Granny Jenny*. The two series were roughly contemporary in their overlap, though the first *Jenny* books were published earlier. There were twenty of them, but just ten of the *Heather Jeans*."

"Oh," Pip said. She wondered if she wanted to investigate these two series. If she did, she might be entertained for months. On the other hand, she might end up completely down the literary rabbit hole.

Jonquil went on, "Other rumoured treasures are older books that were never reprinted, or that came out in tiny editions, or that sold out and the buyers, for some reason, never passed them on.

"Quite often, long series have the first dozen or so books reprinted over and over while the last few never are, and so on. It happened with the *Call of the Glen* series. The final books in that one are so rare they might as well not exist."

"Then how does anyone know what's its name — *Granny Jenny*?" Pip asked.

"It's advertised as *coming soon* on the jacket flap of some of the reprints," Jonquil said.

"I see," Pip said noncommittally. The explanation seemed likely to go on forever, so she thought she'd better stop asking questions. If she decided to pursue the two series she could look them up on-line later.

Jonquil wasn't letting go of the subject yet. *"Grandmother's Sunshine* appears to be one of those legends. I've met a couple of people who say they, or their mother or grandmother, could remember seeing a copy or having it read to them, but it never turns up in the second-hand market or at rare book auctions. I think there must have been *a* book they're remembering, but it's probably one of those mass-produced storybooks from *The Sunshine Series* in the nineteen thirties. Those turn up from time to time, but none of my hopeful customers has ever identified one as *the* book. Not that it happens all that often, thank goodness. One of these days I'm going to sit down and compile a list of apocryphal books and put it on our website, so people know not to waste their time or ours in trying to track them down. I can put up whatever explanations I can theorise. I might even put up a reward for any confirmed sighting of a physical copy . . . though that might give people naughty ideas of forgeries or illegally scanning the ones they might find."

"Never mind then," Pip said hurriedly. "I'll look forward to my *Orders of the Fay.* And if—"

"If I ever see a copy of *Grandmother's Sunshine,* I'll let you know. How did you hear of it, by the way? I try to trace these rumours to their source so I can explain to would-be purchasers where the legend began. As with *Granny Jean* being actually called *Granny Jenny* and coming from another series and by a different author."

Pip said, "My cousin told me our grandmother remembered *her* grandmother having a copy . . . I think."

"That would take it back to the eighteenth or nineteenth century," Jonquil said. "I don't suppose there's photographic evidence. Or a handy catalogue of books owned by the household in . . . of course there isn't. Even if there was, it could easily be a misspelling or a misprint.

"Aside from the ones I mentioned, there's a kind of race memory of a book called *Lutina Domina*. That one sprang from a single mention in an inventory. It turned out to be an old copy of *The Moon is a Lady*. Some idiot had turned it into cod Latin.

"Even now catalogues on books in print often have errors, such as ghost books which had isbns issued but which were never printed—"

"Never mind," Pip said again, but Jonquil still wasn't ready to drop the subject. Apparently it was a cherished hobby horse, and in Pip she thought she'd found a captive audience.

"I had a request for *Grandmother's Sunshine* only a few weeks back, from one of our regular customers. She said she remembered seeing it when she was very young, and having it read to her by someone . . . she thought it was a teacher. She wanted to get a copy to read to her daughter. From the way she described it I'm nearly sure it was an *old* book. Probably much older than *The Sunshine Series*, and now I'm wondering if it might have been a family album, or something like that. Young ladies . . . and older ones . . . used to do botanical sketches and watercolours, and some of those were either passed down through families or else privately printed."

"Maybe," Pip said. She was wondering how to get Jonquil Orange off the line when she remembered *she* was the one who usually hung up.

"I have to go. My agent's come in," she said. "Thanks, Jonquil." She ended the call abruptly.

Magda frowned at her. "What the devil was all that about?"

Pip realised she must have heard only one half of the conversation. "I was ordering books."

"I know that. What was all that *ausflüchte* about that

children's book?"

"The what?"

Magda waggled her hand. "Fibbing. Sidestepping. Prevarication."

"Oh, that." Pip took refuge in vagueness.

"Yes, *that*. You told me plainly that you have a copy of a book called *Grandmother's Sunshine*, but it seems Jonquil Orange was doubting its existence. And what Jonquil Orange doesn't know of books would fit on a pinhead and leave room for the dancing angels."

"You *know* her?"

"It was obviously Jonquil from the Orange Grove. It's not a common name, and I should think most readers with interests outside the best seller list would know of her. Her husband, too, but Jonquil is the one most people deal with. So, why were you asking for a copy of that book when you already have one?"

"I wondered if she'd heard of it."

"And she seems to think it's a chimera. So, why didn't you tell her you *have* a copy instead of fibbing?"

Pip said, "I didn't fib. I said my cousin told me — and so she did. She has a copy, too. I was wishing I'd thought to ask for more information when my grandparents were still with us. Jan said she *had* asked, and that was what Little Nanna Laurel told her. So — I told the perfect truth."

"Hmmm. It's not a lie, or even a lie by omission, but it's definitely dodgy."

Pip narrowed her eyes. She'd been criticised often enough, but she didn't believe she owed Magda any explanations. Their association was new, and she was unsure whether she wanted to pursue it beyond this possible role. She said coolly, "It's a book. My book. Our family books. If I spread it around the book cosmos that we have two family copies of a book so rare it's no more than race memory, we'll have people calling and emailing and annoying us, trying to get us to sell."

"Then why mention it at all, if it's such a big secret?"

"It's not a secret, precisely. And I don't know why I mentioned it. Wait—yes I do! I ordered my books and remembered the shop motto. I just came up with a rare title to see if it was one they could get. In case I ever want to give a copy to someone without sacrificing my own. It's a gorgeous book."

"Hmmm," Magda said, much as Jonquil had done. "You may have a point about spreading information. I won't tell anyone that you have a copy."

"Why would you?"

"If by chance the information creeps out one day, I want you to know it didn't come from me. Mind you, I'd like to see this book. You've made me quite curious."

Pip hit another number on her phone.

Chapter Four. Calling Clarkia

"Now what are you doing?" Magda sounded exasperated. Pip ignored her. "Clarkia?"

"Hello, Pippin. How did the screen test go?"

"The way they usually do, but with less waiting and nicer people. Would you do me a favour?"

"If I can."

"Okay. Go to the bookshelf in the bedroom."

"I'm going . . . right, I'm there."

"Turn on the lamp. Up on the top shelf, on the right-hand side, there are some kids' books. See them?"

"Yes."

"Look for the one called *Grandmother's Sunshine*. It has a pale green spine. I think it's on the end of the shelf because there's no author name." She stopped, recalling that Clarkia probably knew her way around Jan's copy and would recognise Pip's.

"Okay, I have it in my hand. Now what?"

"Lay it on the bed and take a photo of the cover with your phone. Then take a couple of interior spreads, and the inscription page. Then put the book back—unless you want to read it of course, you're welcome to read *anything* in my shelves—and email the pics to me."

"I can do that."

"How are the cats?"

"Devious and possibly demented," Clarkia said.

Pip laughed. "Tell them to *tell no one*."

She hung up.

She turned back to Magda and said, belatedly, "Did you come up for any special reason, or just to tell me my tea was cold and to question me on books?"

Magda rolled her eyes. "I came to tell you I had a call from Jasper Diamond."

"That was quick. Usually they mess you around for weeks."

"They're on a deadline," Magda reminded dryly.

So they were.

"I've decided I'll go to the festival anyway. I want to talk to Matin Campania's wife about cat and dolphin music for my ballet," Pip put in.

"*Gott im Himmel!*" Magda threw up her hands, making her brightly patterned shawl flare out like richly detailed wings. "Pippin Pearmain, you are without a doubt the most exasperating person I've ever had the misfortune to represent!"

"Worse than Peter P?"

"Peter, bless his salty tongue, is a paragon of sweet reason beside you!"

Pip grinned, rather gratified at having made such an impression.

The old girl's still got it . . .

"Think it's funny do you?" Magda glowered at her before suddenly bursting into a hearty bout of laughter. When she'd finished, she said, "In case you're even remotely interested, you got the part of *Solace.*"

Pip wondered if she was glad or disappointed. This part would be in an indie art film at best, but she'd never been exactly mainstream. If it led to a comeback of sorts, her cosy life would be disrupted more often, but then—things had not been the same since the Delmsford Flower Show. She'd felt melancholy and restless even before she had her holiday at the fossmere.

It never occurred to her to back out of the role now she had it. Sully had taught her the value of professionalism.

Magda continued, "Jasper said Humphrey Carpenter-Rivers saw the test and practically tied himself in knots with self-congratulation. He said not to bother testing anyone else. In fact, he said if you weren't cast as Solace, he'd pull out of the deal."

"Oh, good," Pip said, in a tone nicely judged to be halfway between nonchalance and enthusiasm. "That means I can go to the festival without having to hire a car. When do we go?"

"When it starts. Two days' time. It's a crazy schedule, but you won't have lines to learn."

"Two days, eh. That'll work. I have stuff I want to do while we're still here."

Magda cocked her head enquiringly. "Do you need me to do this *stuff*?"

"No, though you're welcome to come with me if you like."

"Come where? When? How?"

"I'm going to a place called the fossmere early tomorrow morning. I'll probably need Edgar or Joan. Someone who can open the gate for me and take me through. What'd you call it? An escort?"

"Escort or pilot." Magda pulled a wry face. "I couldn't do it, I'm afraid. I can't *go*, either, without someone of t' blood, as Edgar puts it, to hold my hand. And I mean that literally."

Pip murmured her understanding. She knew it was possible to travel large distances while holding a fairy's hand. She also knew that letting go, deliberately or by accident, would leave one stranded until or unless the fairy either came back or sent someone else to find one.

Chapter Five. The Fossmere Revisited

Pip arrived at the chalk dancing ground at a few minutes to seven on Friday morning.

Edgar left her there, saying he would visit his friends Master and Mistress Kingsolver and return in time to pilot her home. Seeing a solidly build man in three-quarter pants and a vast loose shirt take three strides and vanish made Pip blink, but she trusted Edgar to return for her. Even if he didn't, the fossmere family would make sure she got back.

She wondered how Jane would react to seeing her unexpectedly and was gratified and touched when the girl's eyes lit up with unfeigned joy.

"Miss Pip! Dadda didn't say you were coming to dance with me again!" Jane gave her a hug, as if she'd been a favoured aunt.

"He didn't know," Pip said, wriggling free. She glanced over at Trae, who was, as usual, consuming figs, and grinned at him.

He grinned back. "Greet you, Miss Pip."

Pip felt everything relaxing into contentment. *Home.* It wasn't, but she was.

"Have either of you two seen a book series called *Orders of the Fay*?"

"Yes," Trae said, through a mouthful.

Jane nodded. "I have, too. I love the pictures, but I wish the author had included humans . . . and the fay cats."

"The fay cats get an entry in volume seven, and humans do get mentioned, along with trace fay and fay-touched," Trae said. He lifted his flute, seeming pleased but unsurprised at Pip's return. "Ready, Miss Pip?"

"Just a moment." Pip raised her voice. "Would you start with "Silk and Circumstance," Trae? If that's all right with Jane?"

Jane expressed herself willing to dance to *anything*.

The boy nodded and launched into the waltz tune.

After limbering up as she normally did, Pip walked through the first part of her ballet, working out the range of the stage. One dancer could judge it easily, but she'd need a *corps de ballet* of sorts to be the dolphins. Maybe a dozen or so?

In her mind's eye she saw a group of children dancing the easy steps she'd blocked out . . . she'd have to teach them precision, though. Just skipping through the daisies like spring lambs wouldn't cut it.

"What's that you're dancing, Miss Pip?" Jane called as they paused for Trae to consume a large slice of honey cake.

Pip realised with a jolt that Jane didn't know anything of *Delphine*. The ballet was so much an accomplished fact in her mind, but she'd conceived the idea only a few days before, during the boat trip with Jules and Tane before they returned her to *Tulpenmanie*. She hadn't spoken with Jane since then, other than this morning.

She didn't feel like explaining the whole thing at present, so she repeated more or less what she'd said to Felicity Dark, the blonde who'd applauded her at the castle. "It's part of a ballet called *Delphine*. It's about—"

"Dolphins!" Jane clasped her hands in her joyful, unself-conscious fashion that ought to have looked twee and precious in a girl of her age. She swung into a beautiful arabesque. "I could *see* them! Can you show me the next part?"

Pip said cautiously that she'd see what she could remember.

Remember isn't all that different from work out . . .

"After the entry of the dolphins, where they dance and

play games, one of them finds a sunken ship," she said. Just saying it aloud firmed the idea even more as a fact.

Then a peculiar thought struck her. "Um—*do* ships sink here?"

"I don't know," Jane said cautiously. "Mostly if one of them gets a hole someone fixes a patch."

Of course they do!

"Well, this one did sink, a long time ago. Maybe it was a really old ship and not worth patching." She sketched the movements and danced in a wide circle.

"The dolphin goes to fetch the others, and they—"

"They swim in and out of the gaps?" Jane supplied.

"Yes. Could you try that out with me?"

They danced through imaginary portholes, and Jane added a few extra bits where she examined items with interest or trepidation.

They tried out a few more sequences, and when they'd finished their hour, then added some more, Jane said, "The dolphin who discovers the ship is a soloist, but is there a principal?"

Pip hesitated. She was fond of Jane, but she'd already decided she wasn't technically good enough for the principal dancer who would lead the narrative, and whose connection with the dolphins she hadn't yet decided. She'd grown more ambitious as the choreography developed.

She was going to prevaricate, but she remembered Magda's reaction to her conversation with Jonquil.

"There will be, but I haven't worked on that part yet. There's also a shark, or maybe a giant squid. Or both."

"Can't you remember?" Jane sounded sympathetic.

Pip gave in. "It's not that I can't remember. It's just that I haven't decided. This is a choreography I'm working out myself."

"It's coming along so well!" Jane said without missing a beat. Maybe, Pip thought, she'd already suspected that.

Jane took Pip's hand. "Let's go to the fossmere. Trae . . ."

"I remember. Camomile tea," the boy said.

The waterfall pool was deserted, so Jane and Pip continued their discussion in the water.

The tea arrived, not with Trae but with Sulane, who poured it out and settled on the bank.

She handed Pip a towel and they sat in the sun.

"Do you dance, Sulane?" Pip asked.

"Sometimes I go to ceilidhs, but I don't do ballet," the girl said. "I have other things I like to do. Are you coming back tomorrow, Miss Pip?"

"Yes, if that's all right."

"It's *always* all right," Jane said emphatically. "I love having someone to practise with. I love talking ballet. Laura does, too, and Ammie, sometimes, but Sulane and Trae aren't interested, and the others are too little."

"As long as Edgar can bring me through the castle bridge gate again, I'll be here," Pip said.

Sulane said, "Jane's Ardal will come to fetch you with a pony, if you want."

Pip saw an opportunity to get in a request to learn jumping. She agreed like a shot.

She was dressed by the time Edgar returned. He greeted the sisters with good cheer but no obvious recognition and took Pip's hand. "Will you want to come back here tomorrow, Miss Pip?"

Pip explained Sulane's offer of Ardal.

"That'll be one of t' Cornfellow lads. Grand! I'll just let you through t' gate then, and hand you into his care," he said.

Pip reflected that everything fell into place for her in these lovely surroundings. It was magic, she supposed.

"If it's all right with Ardal," she added, realising his time and ponies might not be Sulane's to promise.

Jane and Sulane, and even Edgar, exchanged slightly

puzzled glances. Why wouldn't it be all right with Ardal? They didn't voice the thought, but it seemed to hover in the air.

Pip, with whom requests had often *not* been *all right*, because they'd been inconvenient or just plain unwanted, felt unworthy.

Who was it who'd said recently that she felt she should have been better? Ah, it was Jillian, and she'd been speaking of Zach, temporary skipper of *Tulpenmanie*. Zach was kind, patient, generous and transparent. Pip reflected that she was not necessarily any of these things. But then, Jisinia wasn't either, and Zach seemed pretty devoted to her. Possibly they were complementary.

She remembered the leprechaun woman, Branna Pusheen, sending that message to Jisinia. Something about wanting Jin to come and see her before she took the Paddy . . . Paddy something. She frowned. *Paddy* might be the name of a leprechaun man, or it could be a slang word for someone in a temper . . . What had that to do with Jisinia?

"Ready, lass?" Edgar's voice broke into her pondering.

"Yes. Bye, Jane and Sulane. I'll see you in the morning. Thank Trae for me."

Just before she and Edgar stepped into the familiar blue, Pip saw the sisters exchange another glance. *Why thank Trae? He'd be playing for Jane anyway . . .*

"Edgar, what's a paddy?" Pip asked.

"I know a few leppy men with that name. Patsys, too. Paddy Songstitch, now, and Paddy Painter. Paddy Castle's another of them. Patsy Weaver sometimes gets called Paddy. Was that what you meant?"

"I think it was a what, not a who."

"Then I doubt I can help thee." Edgar sounded regretful. "Unless t' *Orders* book has owt to say on it? Seems to me I might remember something . . ."

Back at the guesthouse, Pip drank her customary lemon

and water.

She consulted Volume Seven of *The Orders of the Fay* and ran rapidly through the first few entries for P.

Paddy Cèilidh—a leprechaun dance. No. *Paddy Chalice*. That rang a bell.

Pip learned it was a jewelled chalice, or cup, used for celebratory draughts of poteen. Evidently many leprechaun families had one and it was passed down the generations.

That left her little the wiser. Jisinia wasn't a leprechaun, surely?

Having rinsed her cup and tidied her hair, Pip went back downstairs, where she encountered Joan Treadwell, a tall, solid woman who wore a comfortable loose sweater, well-worn jeans, and a string of pearls.

Joan said she was going to the shops and asked if Pip needed a lift anywhere.

Just as if we were neighbours who'd known one another for years!

Pip pounced on the opportunity to ask for a ride back to the Fairy Gardens. She wanted to consolidate the new sequences she'd worked on with Jane, and the grassy stage at the gardens would be perfect.

Joan agreed that would be easy, and Edgar, whose hearing Pip thought must be uncommonly good, appeared from the kitchen five minutes later with sandwiches, parkin, and a pear in a neat paper bag.

Magda accompanied Pip to Windhill, saying she planned to call on Pandora's mother and stepfather *to see how they matched up to their statues*.

Pip hoped, with no confidence whatsoever, that Magda would *not* start a discussion upon the definition of a dad.

Having parted from Joan and Magda at the Founders' Gate, she paid her respects to the statues, gloating in anticipation over her beautiful bucket-to-be. She hoped Xavier Partridge would soon get off the galleon and be available for her request. The alarming Frances had seemed to think he'd comply, and since she was answering his phone, she must have some idea of his schedule.

She set off down the path, and after a few missed turns, found her way to the natural stage near the outdoor chapel where she'd danced the day before.

She was unreasonably annoyed to find it already occupied by what looked to her cranky gaze like two dozen women and at least thirty dogs.

CHAPTER SIX. CADDY

Pip stared with displeasure at the sea of dogs and women. Were dogs allowed in the Fairy Gardens?

Didn't they have designated dog parks to swarm in? With high mesh fences to keep them off public spaces and to contain their balls and sticks and other doggy accoutrements?

And weren't you planning to become a better person?

Maybe sixty-six was too old for self-improvement.

Must ask Magda.

From years of omnivorous reading, Pip had the impression the Spanish flu pandemic had ended in around 1920. She certainly hadn't studied it at school, but it had featured in some historical novels she'd read.

If Magda's father had died in that epidemic, she must have been born no more than nine months later. Pip discounted any idea of frozen sperm or any such tinkering. It followed that Magda's claim to be older than Sully was probably true.

She would be over one hundred, although she didn't look more than seventy, so it was no wonder she'd referred to Pip as a spring chicken.

Did Magda see herself as a work in progress? She certainly hadn't folded her hands and resigned herself to God's waiting room—just look at her taking-over of the moribund Sullivan Gilbert agency! She had the energy of a woman less than half her age.

Pip knew she could go somewhere else to work on her dolphin ballet, but she'd had her heart set on her Fairy Gardens stage. She felt her bottom lip protrude and dragged herself and her sulky inner child into line.

They might go soon.

She leaned against a tree and watched for signs of packing up. Then she concentrated her attention on the group. *Go. Go on, go home.*

The women were in small groups of two or three, sitting on the grass or strolling in pairs, watching their dogs at play. Some of them were throwing balls or combing their pets, but mostly they were socialising while the dogs did likewise.

A woman in a tight yellow dress was laughing with two fair young women. They all wore a good deal of silver jewellery and they all had babies or toddlers in slings.

Pip stared at them. They were so, so foreign to her, and yet, with all that flashing adornment, they reminded her of Tane and Jillian.

A Jack Russell, a Scottie and an odd little mixed dog were disposed at their feet. The Jack rested like a Trafalgar lion, while the other two were bouncing and roughhousing.

As Pip watched, the mixed dog snarled shrilly and nipped the Scottie, who switched sideways and put a heavy paw on the aggressor's head.

One of the blondes leaned over to examine the situation and the other women crowded in closer.

A football huddle? Do footballers huddle?

Pip narrowed her eyes as she saw them rearrange their formation as a man joined them from . . . somewhere. He was tall with floppy black hair, and he put his arm around one of the women and kissed her baby.

His baby, Pip supposed. To her unpractised eye it looked to be the youngest of the three children.

The man was laughing, and actually shaking a finger at the mixed dog. "Take that, you fiend."

"Mull, *must* you?" the yellow-clad woman said.

The man stretched in a manner that suggested an excellent opinion of his rights and skills. "Can't let the Attapeke get above his nasty little self. If Shelley won't discipline him, the Douglas will."

The woman picked up the small dog, which looked unchastened. Her baby, really more of a small child, reached out of the sling to grab the dog's ear.

Trouble!

Pip's instant thought was mistaken. The little dog wagged its tail and tried to lick the child's face.

Pip saw the Jack Russell eyeing the dog and the baby with the intensity of her breed, while the Scottie was — nowhere.

Pip's mind did a triple take as she put together what she'd seen with how her brain interpreted the events and added what she'd learned from Jamie Pendennis.

It's more common in men.

That Scottie dog is — that man. That Scottie dog is like Jamie's Kakao.

A surge of smugness ran over her.

You might be young and beautiful people, and you might have babies and probably magic talents, and delightful futures, but I know something you don't know I know.

Oops . . . Must not be smug. Hastily, she switched to hoping, as patiently as she could, that they'd decide to go and buy kippers or something. Surely those babies ought to be having their naps at home.

She watched the little sub-group for a while, but they didn't leave, and the Scottie didn't reappear. She decided they were family in some degree.

An upright woman with curly white hair must have seen her interest, because she came up with an equally white curly dog trotting beside her.

"Good morning!"

"Hello," Pip said cautiously. She offered the back of her hand to the white dog, which gave her a friendly sniff.

"This is Mary-Mary," the woman said. "Do you have dogs?"

Pip shook her head. "I live with three cats."

"Oh, dear. You're the opposition."

"I'm not opposed to dogs."

Except when they occupy the space I want to use and that's really down to the owners.

She added, "I like dogs. The cats had a visiting dog a while back." She remembered Jamie's self-description. "He is a respectable dog. Civilised. I see your Mary-Mary is, too."

The woman smiled ruefully. "I beg your pardon. I'm afraid we—" she indicated the assorted women and dogs "—tend to assume everyone is a cynophile or else a cynophobe. In my defence you *were* looking a tad annoyed, or acquisitive . . .or maybe covetous is the right word. Which of the dogs is your heart's desire?"

Pip said, "None of them. I'm sure they're all lovely dogs, but I covet the space."

"Um . . ."

She clarified, "Your group, or club or whatever you are is occupying my dancing space."

The woman looked taken aback, as most people did when interacting with Pip for the first time.

Pip said testily, "I *know* there are other places to dance, but I'm choreographing a ballet, and this spot has perfect ambiance. I did some blocking here the other day and I wanted to reinforce it. I have a spatial awareness problem and I use visual cues . . . oh, never mind."

The woman bit her bottom lip. "I'm afraid you were unlucky . . ." She looked questioning.

"I'm Pippin Pearmain," Pip said.

The woman's face lit into a grin. "Ah. The asset my sister drove to an audition yesterday while under the thrall of the inimitable Magda Quest Saxer."

"Screen test," Pip corrected, then she said with more attention, "Pandora is your sister?"

"Yes. And it's a testament to Magda's force of personality

that she has Panda playing chauffeur for her. Until Magda showed up in our lives, I'd have said *no one* could get Panda to do anything she didn't want to, but maybe that's just a younger sister's distorted view of the elder.

"I'm Carolyn Hildebrand. Caddy, if you like. If you're thinking Panda and I don't look alike, that's easily explained. I take after Mum, and she looks like her dad. Our brother looks like Dad *and* Mum, which is quite an achievement."

"So those statues at the gate are your parents," Pip said, stopping the flood of revelation. Why did people always think she wanted to know their life histories and their pedigrees?

"Yes. Panda provided a photo of them in the nineteen fifties, taken before Jakin and I were born. Xavier got a wonderful likeness, not only in form and pose but in personality. They — you know how it's often said one person *loves* and the other *is loved* in a relationship? It works out beautifully for Mum and Dad. Dad fell in love with Mum when she was fifteen and he was just a bit older. Before he could propose to her, or ask her to go steady, she went off to art school. He used to visit her there sometimes. When she came back, he gave her a pair of red rose earrings as a Christmas present. Red roses for love triumphant, you know. *Really* making a statement."

Pip nodded. The language of flowers was second nature to someone from the Laurel-Pearmain-de-Leon family.

"She gave *him* a painting she'd done of him and her brother when they were young, and she'd incorporated the red rose he gave her back then in their teens. The symbolism seems straightforward, but the more you think of it, the more complex it becomes. They've been married for seventy-three years." A shadow passed over her face. "I don't know what will happen when one of them goes."

Pip said, "The other will go on."

"You sound as if you have experience."

"I've seen it happen five times." Pip explained the big and little nannas and pops, Little Mum and Little Dad and Aunt Helen and Uncle Lance de Leon.

"Little Mum was the last one left, and she was *all right*. She really was. We went on doing things, cooking and gardening, and watching old films. She kept Little Dad's things in place, with his jacket on its peg and his favourite cup on its shelf by the milk jug, as if he was just around the corner. I think he probably was . . . to her. He never was very noisy. Neither was Little Mum. They could sit there quite contentedly, reading, or playing solitaire or whatever, and every so often they'd have a few quiet words."

That struck her suddenly as strange. Little Nanna Pearmain and both Little Pops and Little Mum and Dad had all been quiet and gentle people. Only Little Nanna Laurel had shown great force of character, managing people without apparent effort. If Schizanthus Laurel said *frog*, people, even Big Nanna de Leon, hopped. Pip had used to wonder if she was a witch — of the *good* variety, obviously.

Caddy blew out her cheeks. "That makes such good sense. I see Mum *will* be all right if she's the one left. She kept up her painting and drawing after art school. She still does a bit of illustration, although she's the first to say she's not top class. She says being a jobbing artist is nothing to be ashamed of, and because she's self-employed, she never had to retire."

Pip nodded emphatically. She understood that being a jobbing performer and being no more than competent at ballet had not diminished her zeal and enjoyment.

Chapter Seven. Dames with Dogs

Caddy bent to rub her dog's head, and the movement released a soft scent of violets. Pip sniffed appreciatively.

"I love that perfume. Violet Veritas, isn't it? I still have the last bottle Little Mum bought fifteen or so years ago. I didn't think they made it anymore."

An odd expression flitted over Caddy's face and vanished, leaving her smiling gently.

"I remember the perfume you mean, but I'm not wearing it. It was a lovely one, much more realistic than most."

Pip got the *I know something* feeling again.

You're a fay . . . well, half one. Your dad is an elf.

She said, "You were saying I was unlucky about the dogs being here . . . Why would you think that, since you're a member of the group?"

"Was I—oh yes. Mostly we meet at the dog park, but they're doing some construction there and we can't hear ourselves think, so we've relocated here for a couple of weeks."

"We?"

"Us. Yes. We are a group, as you supposed. We're the Dames with Dogs. Some of them, anyway. I doubt if we've ever *all* been to a gathering at the same time.

"It's all pretty casual. No dues, no exclusions . . . the only thing you need to have to join is either a dedicated dog or the earnest intention to obtain one in the near future."

"What of him?" Pip gestured to the dark-haired man she'd decided was a part-time Scottie. He had acquired his baby from its mother.

"Well, he has a dedicated dog," Caddy said, with what Pip considered a masterful sidestep. "His mum sometimes comes, although she's not a regular member. His foster sister, Elfie, is our club artist. She's not here today, or I'd introduce you. She'd *love* to paint you. All that said, Mull's not an actual member either, more of an affiliate."

"Men can't be members?" Pip wondered how the dames got away with making that rule.

"It's a very interesting point. We are *dames,* which implies women, but from about eighteen-oh-six, pantomime dames have been portrayed by men. We think that fact will allow us to let a man join if one ever wants to. We could get a ruling from the chairwoman and committee . . . if we had one. And we can point it out if anyone decides to make trouble."

She glanced at her watch. "We'll be out of your hair soon. Some of us have children or grandchildren to deal with. Then there's lunch to prepare, and — well, let's say members tend to be heavily involved in lots of things. It's said that if you're not busier than the day is long, then you're probably not a member of Dames with Dogs."

Pip turned her attention to the white dog, Mary-Mary. She was an odd-looking animal, more like a sheep than a dog. Pip decided to try a little Cat-Morse. After all, it had worked on Patchwork Nora when she visited the village at Smile o' the Glean.

"Do you like cheese, Mary-Mary?" She said it aloud and thought it too for good measure.

The dog looked up with intelligent brown eyes, but there was no answer echoing in Pip's mind.

No Dog-Morse then? Or does she just not do it with strangers?

Caddy said, "She likes cheese, but I don't give it to her too often. I take it you have some. If so, she can probably smell it."

Pip removed a cheese sandwich from her messenger bag. It was part of the carry-out lunch Edgar had provided. "May

I?"

Caddy said, "Yes . . . but only a corner."

Mary-Mary accepted the treat with gentle courtesy.

"She's got better manners than Kittisack and Amberjill," Pip said. "The cats, I mean."

She turned to scan the other dogs and women. The Dog-Morse experiment had failed with Mary-Mary, but that didn't mean the theory was wrong.

Caddy, apparently noticing she was dismissed, took herself and Mary-Mary off so smoothly it might have been rehearsed. Pip gave her top marks. Ending conversations in person was sometimes as awkward as it had been to get Jonquil Orange off the phone. One or more of the parties would linger when it was obviously time to go.

The Scottie-man and his harem had gone elsewhere, so Pip scanned the wider group to find a likely subject. She talked to the cats at home as a matter of course, but usually she addressed them directly by name or designation. With the dogs at the Fairy Gardens she didn't know names, apart from Mary-Mary's, and she doubted if they'd respond to *hey, you, fluffy dog with the long nose* . . . She walked into the dancing area, strolling along as if looking for someone . . . which she was.

A middle-aged woman in an orange skirt gave her a questioning look. She had a baby sling, but no baby. Instead, she had an aged chihuahua luxuriating in her lap with a faded toy, and two tiny puppies playing hide and seek in the full folds of her skirt.

Pip had always rather liked chihuahuas because they reminded her of herself. Like her, they were often underestimated.

"Are they all related?" she asked.

The woman said, "The pups are. Pepe—that's our old man—is going to be an impossible act to follow." She blinked and a look of sorrow passed over her face. "Anyway . . . these two ragamuffins aren't his relations. Meet José and Juan—they're fostering with us for a while. If we start to feel like family, they will stay. If not, then my daughter will take them into her menagerie." She fished in her skirt and pulled out one of the pups, which she dumped into her lap along with the old dog.

He lifted his head and nudged the baby with his faded muzzle.

The pup rolled over, exposing a fat tummy and soft new paws.

"Hello, Pepe," Pip said.

He focused his milky eyes on her.

"You like these pups?" she asked.

Pepe didn't exactly answer, but a feeling came over her that he was pleased the pups were there. *My legacy* was the impression she got, and the feeling was proud and contented.

"What?" The woman looked suddenly interested.

Pip said, cautiously, "I *think* he thinks of them as being his, somehow."

Pepe's mistress blinked again. "That's odd. I've sometimes had the same impression. They're not, though. No chance."

Pip sought for an explanation. "Maybe he feels as if he's somehow paved the way for them . . . he's their godfather, or their sponsor."

"You might be right. I hope so." The woman looked up, her eyes glazing a bit. "Pepe's lived with us longer than even a chi usually manages, but he's fading now. He's not ill, or in pain, he's just *tired*. Wearing out. The vet said to let him do what he wants . . . and that he'll let us know when he's had enough. Bri and I—that's my husband—wondered if we could bear to get another dog, but our daughter came up with the idea that we might foster these two *now*. If they upset our old man, she'd take them. He seems pleased, though. We got two so they'd play together and not pester him."

"I think that's wonderful. He knows he's leaving you in good hands . . . or do I mean paws?"

The little old dog closed his eyes, but his tail wagged a few times.

"Could I hold him?" Pip ventured.

The woman half raised the puppy, but Pip gestured to the old dog.

"Yes, if you like. You'll have to take the stuffie too. He never does anything without the stuffie."

Pip received an armful of old dog and decrepit stuffed toy.

She bent and kissed the tiny domed head. Unlike a lot of old dogs, Pepe smelled fresh. He clearly had the best care anyone could provide.

Pip whispered, "When you go to glory, you look out for Little Mum. Her name's Rosie Pearmain and she and Little Dad Jon will *love* you. You can live with them and play in the big garden they'll have made. You might look up Lupin too . . ."

She kissed him again and handed him back.

"Remember, find Rosie, and Jon . . . and maybe Lupin. Share the love." She nodded to the woman. "He's so lucky!"

Then she wandered off.

Her efforts at Dog-Morse remained inconclusive until she encountered the black spaniel bitch.

The dog sat alone near the chapel with her front paws neatly crossed in front of her.

She looked at Pip in mild surprise as she approached.

Pip said, "I don't suppose *you* speak Dog-Morse?"

The spaniel tilted her head so one dangling ear brushed the ground, but no thought came from her to Pip.

"Didn't think so." Pip looked for a putative owner, but the dog seemed to be on her own. She had no collar, unless it was hidden under the lush mane of fur, but she couldn't possibly be a stray. Her eyes were an odd colour.

"Dog-Morse?" Pip repeated.

She put a hand out to stroke the dog, but something in those eyes suggested she'd better not.

Pip was impressed. She'd perfected just that same steely look to depress the pretentions of people who encroached because she was small, and they mistook diminutive size for weakness.

"You're a formidable thing," she said. "Do you really bite, or is that *look* enough?"

She sat down next to the dog. "I live with three cats. Two of them are fay cats and the third one is a kind of guardian made of pottery. They communicate with me in Cat-Morse. I was hoping you might know Dog-Morse. If you do, give me a sign. Three blinks will do."

The dog looked bored and began preening her paws.

Go away, do, and leave me to my toilette, her pose implied, but that was all.

Pip watched. "You're just a grumpy ordinary dog. With those eyes, I hoped you were a fay dog."

Someone laughed nearby.

Chapter Eight. Dog-Talk

Pip looked up into a face she'd seen before . . . almost. She frowned. It *was* or maybe it *wasn't* the man she'd seen with the three women with babies.

She cleared her throat. *Was? Wasn't?* Wasn't, probably. Despite the laugh, this one didn't look so smug.

"Lots of people talk to dogs," she stated.

"Undoubtedly," he said.

"Is this dog yours?"

"No, I'm hers."

"I hope you're not being *winsome,*" Pip said. "I don't know what you've been told about getting in touch with your feminine side, but I'm here to tell you *winsome* doesn't cut it if you're a man. Unless you're practising being a Dame?"

The man uttered a snort of laughter. "You sound like my mother."

"I'm nobody's mother."

"I bet you're a damned effective aunt."

"I'm not that, either."

His amusement stopped abruptly. "I'm sorry."

"No need to be *sorry.* It's not your fault. I never had a chance to do the aunt thing, because I'm an only child, but I could have been a mother, maybe, if I'd made an effort." She shrugged. Because he still looked sad for her, she added, "My cousin's daughter is finding sanctuary at my cottage, so at least I can do that."

The young man sat down on the other side of the spaniel bitch, which turned and gave him a long, disgruntled look.

95

He said, "Do you often talk to dogs you don't know?"

"Mostly, I talk to cats I *do* know. I live with three of them—Kittisack, Amberjill, and Lupin's cat."

"Do they talk back?"

Pip quite saw he was humouring the little old lady, so she gave him a verbal jab. "They certainly do. Not in human speech, but in something I call Cat-Morse. I was trying to see if this dog knows Dog-Morse, or whatever the equivalent is. She didn't answer me, so either she's just a plain old dog, or else she's not got good manners. Someone should have taken care of that."

The young man pulled his lip to the side, as if he was trying not to laugh.

Pip had the bit between her teeth. She had always been an intuitive performer, and this was a performance of sorts. She pulled up all her limpid innocence and asked, "Are you sometimes a Scottish terrier?"

That wiped the smile off his face.

"No, of course not. Are you a surrealist, or just nuts?"

"Neither. And there's no *of course*. If you're not a part-time Scottie, I bet you have a brother or a cousin who is. I *saw* him and he looked a lot like you. And before you call the folk in white coats to persuade me I'm daft, I know what I saw is possible because I have a friend who is sometimes a dog."

That got a genuine smile. "If you know a mutie . . . that's what we generally call ourselves . . . why the charade just now?"

"It's not a charade. Two of the cats I live with are fay cats—at least, they didn't deny it when I interrogated them. I assume there are also fay dogs, and this is the biggest concentration of dogs I've come across lately. I got a bit of a glimmer from an old chihuahua, but the rest of the bunch seem to be just dogs. Except for the Scottie, I mean, and I didn't get the chance of a crack at him." She frowned at him. "You told me you *weren't* the Scottie, but you also said *we*, so what are you?"

"A doxie," he said dryly. "And no, I won't show you. He's see-through, and some of the other dogs find him disconcerting." He turned his attention to the spaniel. "Lady Vee, a bit of help here?"

The dog gave him a disgusted look.

"Please?"

The dog turned the look on Pip, who returned it with interest.

The spaniel got to her feet and stretched, morphing into a handsome woman in her forties. She wore a jade-green sweater that Pip immediately coveted, black leggings, and a collection of silver rings and bracelets. Her dark hair was threaded with silver strands, and when she turned her exasperated gaze on Pip, her eyes were the same colour as the dog's.

"Great bogle, woman, but you're persistent! How have you lived to be however old you are without someone taking measures to stop you?"

"I'm fast on my feet," Pip responded. She looked from the woman to the young man. They were alike in colouring and in feature. "I take it he's *yours*? Literally?"

"He was, until I palmed him off on the first woman who'd take him."

"That's a lie," the man said, *sotto voce*. "I found Githa all by myself."

"Dahlia found her," the woman muttered.

Pip went on staring. "Jamie said most of you dog-people were men."

"Who's Jamie?"

"A friend. He drove me to the coast and back and cat-sat while I was away. He's *lovely*."

She hoped that implied that they possibly weren't in Jamie's league.

"He's the mutie you know?" the young man said. "What's his mani? His dog-self, I mean?"

Pip countered, "Am I allowed to tell you? I don't want to do anything wrong, culturally speaking. For all I know, he might belong to a different clan or be a hereditary enemy or something. I don't want to be responsible for starting the Battle of the Baskervilles."

"We don't have hereditary enemies. You can tell us his name because we're already in the loop," the young man said. "We tend to know one another, at least by reputation, and I assure you by whatever you hold holy, that we mean and will do *no harm*."

His mother nodded. "Indeed. *No harm.* And we *do* tend to know of one another. It helps to know where the gene falls so we can choose to reinforce it or try to eradicate it from our lines."

"Ma spent some time seeking a suitable mutie strain to marry into, but in the end she settled for a recessive that she hoped would reinforce in her offspring," the young man said. "I believe my father advertised in the *Bitches' Weekly* and Ma answered his ad."

Pip gave him a hard stare. He looked perfectly serious, which suggested he was trying to annoy his mother.

She refused to buy into intergenerational sniping, so she said, "Jamie's dog looks like an unclipped poodle, sort of chocolate brown. He calls it Kakao."

The man glanced at his mother. "You know that one, Ma?"

"He's not from the Teague line, but he could possibly be a Pendennis offshoot."

That suggested they *were* being truthful. Pip said, "His surname is Pendennis, and he said his dad and his grandad had dog-selves too."

The woman nodded. "Yes, he's most likely one of that clan. They're connected with my husband's family."

Pip folded her arms. "Why didn't you answer me when I was trying to use Dog-Morse?"

"Because I've never heard of Dog-Morse. I certainly can't do it. I'm not a fay dog. Fay dogs don't talk to people anyway."

"Fay cats do."

"Not in my experience."

Her son said, "Ma, they probably communicate with her because she's . . . whatever she is."

"I'm human," Pip said.

"I expect you're right, but there's something definitely odd about you."

"Says the boy who turns into a see-through dachshund and whose mum is a grumpy spaniel."

He winced. "Fay cats *over here* in the human realm occasionally attach themselves to a human, but it's always their own idea."

That accounted pretty well with Pip's experience, but she had other things on her mind now.

"Why didn't you answer me?" she persisted, staring down the part-time-spaniel.

The woman pursed her lips. "I couldn't."

"You understood me, though."

"Up to a point. Domesticated dogs understand some speech, via a complex mix of body language, scent, posture, tone, and sound. It's not just one thing in isolation though, it's the whole package. When I'm—"

"Dogged-out," Pip supplied, quoting Jamie.

"*I* prefer to say *manifested as Lady Velvet,* but when that happens, I use canine perception. My human personality sits back and tunes out, except for a bit of peripheral attention which I use to keep safe from—"

"People like me," Pip suggested.

"I doubt if there *are* other people like you. It's not in

Velvet's best interests to get too friendly with strangers, especially when she is apparently unsupervised." She gave her son a meaningful look. "In any case, when I return to this dominant form, I can look back and interpret what I saw and heard when I was using Lady Velvet's perception. It won't be very useful, though. Velvet is more interested in resting and enjoying the scents and the sunshine than in trying to communicate with strangers which might lead to something unfortunate."

"Oh."

Oho. So Mister Handsome here was supposed to be acting owner for Lady Vee, and instead he was just enjoying the show.

Pip was disappointed. All that effort and she still had no idea if Dog-Morse was a thing.

Still, she had met some more muties.

CHAPTER NINE. GUESSING GAMES

Pip decided to turn the situation to her advantage. "To prevent me from bothering any others like you, will you point out the muties and the fay dogs in this group?" She borrowed from their playbook and added, "I don't mean them any harm."

The woman cast her gaze around. "I can't see any fay dogs present. There *is* one who often comes to gatherings, a little harlequin called Puffin, but she's not here today."

"Any more like you?"

The woman didn't answer, but her son said, "To the best of my knowledge, the only muties here today are Ma, my brother, my wife, and myself. There might be others, but I wouldn't necessarily know. I'm not a member of the Dames, although I regard some of them as friends. Ma? Do you know if there are any others?"

"I haven't enquired into pedigrees," the woman said. "I'm not exactly a member either. I used to come to keep watch over my son's manifestation, mostly in case of Animal Control turning up unannounced and checking microchips. Needless to say, the Black Douglas doesn't have one.

"These days, it's his wife's job to play owner and to get him out of the way of the chip wand, but I still come along. It allows Lady Velvet to enjoy the company of other dogs without it being too obvious. If it's any of your business."

Pip knew it wasn't, really, but she reiterated that she meant no harm. "Personal research," she offered. She added, with only slight sarcasm, "I'm not going to write a learned treatise on people who turn into dogs. Who'd believe me?"

"We would," the young man pointed out. He still looked entertained.

His mother frowned at Pip and said abruptly. "You look familiar. Do I know you from somewhere?"

"As in do you regularly appear on *Australia's Daftest*?" the son asked.

The woman waved her hand at him in an irritable fashion. "You look familiar, but as I don't watch reality trash, it can't be from that."

"Ma, remember, not everyone wants their possible platform referred to as *trash*." There was an edge to the young man's voice, and the woman looked discomforted.

Pip broke in, "I doubt if we've ever met before. I'm from Tasmania. I flew to Sydney a couple of days ago, but until recently I hadn't left home for ten years or more – unless you count a trip to the flower show."

The young man clicked his fingers. "Got it! *Aussie Hermits*."

Pip stared him down. Then something occurred to her. "I don't do *reality*, daft, hermit or otherwise, but you *might* have seen me on TV or in a play. It would have been made or staged a good while ago, but sometimes things get repeated on retro channels."

The woman drew in her brows. Then she snapped her fingers as her son had, making her bracelets chime. "My God, you're Marigold Heriot!"

The young man rolled his eyes up and clasped his hands in mimed ecstasy. "She is! Holy cow! How amazing! How – how –" He dropped back to his normal demeanour to add, "Who the hell is Marigold Heriot?"

His mother said, "There was a film called *The House of Heriot* – a kind of costume drama from the seventies that was a cult favourite, especially among our people. Alain Barfleur was in it and so was *she*. I think."

"Alain *Barfleur!*" The hands clasped again. "Splendiferous! A legend! Who the —"

His mother gave him a sharp poke in the ribs. "Zennor, sometimes you're almost as annoying as your brother."

Zennor?

Pip asked with interest, "What's *your* name? Your first name, I mean? Not planning to stalk you on the socials."

The woman looked disconcerted.

"You couldn't. Ma wouldn't know a social if it pulled her tail," Zennor stated.

His mother ignored that. "My name's Gillan. Note the hard G. It's spelled like Gillian-with-a-G but minus the second I."

Pip considered the information she'd picked up from *Orders of the Fay.* So far, she'd really studied only the alpenfee, and a bit about the braefolk. The alpenfee had German-style names and the braes used Scottish ones.

So, Gillan, Zennor and . . . what was the other one's name?

"What about your brother's name?" she asked Zennor.

"Mullion," Zennor said.

"And your wife? His wife? The woman in the yellow dress?"

He grinned at her, and recited, "Githa is the love of my life, Morgana is my brother's affair . . . do *not* mess with Morgana! The other one is called Dahlia. Don't mess with her, either. She's rackety."

"The babies?"

"Madoc, Daffodil and —" He paused.

Pip said crossly, "I'm still not really getting it. You're not alpenfee or braefolk."

Zennor said, "My daughter is called Camelot. Does that help?"

"Cornish?"

The woman, Gillan, asked, "Why are you playing guessing games?"

Zennor said, "Keep up, Ma. It's obvious Marigold has got

her hands on a copy of *Orders of the Fay*." He added to Pip, "Ma *loves* that series. She keeps buying copies and bestowing them on her friends. By now she's probably single-handedly paid for the print-run of the second edition. I'd say you're part way through the first volume and haven't cracked volume seven yet. Am I right?"

"Yes," Pip said begrudgingly. She didn't like to be predictable. "Aside from looking up P for Paddy."

"As in Paddy Chalice, I assume. I wonder —"

"And now you're trying to use nomenclature to identify our order," Gillan broke in.

"Yes. But Cornish names . . . and I don't think Daffodil and Dahlia fit the picture . . . don't help much. The silver is more of a give-away. I think you're probably piskies."

Zennor applauded silently.

"You're right in what you said of Dahlia and Daffodil, though," the woman said unexpectedly. "Dahlia's mother is human, and her man is an elf. *He* picked their baby's name, so they didn't follow the general pisky naming pattern."

Pip beamed. She'd extracted information from the close-mouthed Gillan. Besides, Dahlia and Daffodil sounded fine names to her. At least she could spell them.

"So, Marigold . . ." Zennor said, eyeing her with obvious interest.

His mother shook her head. "*Her* name's not Marigold. Marigold Heriot was the character she played in *House of Heriot*. And to answer your question, Alain Barfleur —"

"He played the highwayman," Pip interrupted. She added, "My real name is Pippin Pearmain. Pippin Picotee Pearmain, if you want the whole thing. My cousin is Juniper Gin . . . the novelist." She thought she might as well give Jan a plug. She added, "If you buy a copy of her new book, *Garterstakes,* I can ask her to sign it for you."

Zennor clicked his fingers again. "So that's why you're

wandering here and there trying to communicate with dogs. You're an actor, and you're playing a werebitch in your next film!"

Pip eyed him blandly. "Nice try, dog-man. I haven't played a bitch, were or otherwise—yet."

She wondered if the director would let her borrow a dog ... no, a stuffed toy dog, because it would have to last sixty years ... for the film. She could interact with it.

She glanced around at the Dames with Dogs. Despite what Caddy Hildebrand had told her, they looked settled in for the foreseeable future.

She decided to relocate and come back later.

"You're leaving?" Zennor asked.

"Yes. Thank you for the information. I'll come back later to practise my ballet when it's less populated. I'm sorry I bothered you. I'm told I can be annoyingly persistent."

She headed off towards the ocean outlook she'd seen the day before, but somehow she wound up in a grotto.

It reminded her a little of her beautiful fossmere, and she felt a surge of pleasure.

I'm going back there tomorrow morning. I get to ride Fimber and dance with Jane again. I get to swim in the fossmere.

She settled on a natural stone seat and took her feint-lined pad out of her messenger bag. She had information to write down and some notations to confirm. That should fill in the time nicely while she waited for the Dames and their dogs to leave her dancing stage.

Chapter Ten. The Hamper

When Pip returned to the natural stage an hour and a half later, she found it deserted, except for a covered basket resting where she'd conversed with Gillan and her son.

She approached it with caution. She definitely didn't want to find an abandoned puppy.

But those Dames would never do that.

She was sure even the preternaturally prickly Gillan would come over fierce-mother-bitch if a puppy needed her help.

She dabbed the basket with her fingertip, then gave it a little shove. Upon receiving no response, she undid the latch, keeping her face well clear in case —

In case *what*, precisely? Pip pondered, and finally realised she was expecting a swarm of grumpy bees to emerge.

Why —

She laughed. It was one of the pickles Polly Pickle had got into in a seven-part television serial she'd filmed back in the late 1960s. She'd been fourteen, but so small and slight it was easy to cast her as the nine-year-old titular character. Polly had been an impulsive but good-hearted child who rescued those who didn't want it, assisted those who didn't need it, and otherwise got into pickles through no intended fault of her own. In the episode Pip was remembering she'd accidentally mixed up her aunt's picnic basket with a beekeeper's skip . . .

There were no bees in the basket today.

Pip peeped in with caution.

Inside was a bunch of marigolds in various shades of

yellow, orange, and rust, calendula *and* tagetes, a couple of apples, a covered flask, something wrapped in a napkin, and an elegant envelope. The marigolds were in a pretty glass vase, tied with a fine silver cord, and everything was padded with what she first assumed to be a tablecloth, but which turned out to be a dress-length in a riot of marigold colours.

A hamper, then. For her?

Pip poked at the apples. One was small and pear-shaped, and the other round and streaked. Her eyebrows went up as she recognised a pearmain and a Cox's Orange pippin.

Someone knows their fruit.

She opened the envelope, remembering the one Lupin had left for her, which had led to such a change in her life.

If I hadn't had my Experience I might not have had the courage to accept Magda's offer. I wouldn't have had my ballet, and the film, and I wouldn't have met Jane or the Dames. I wouldn't have danced at the fossmere, and I wouldn't be here right now.

Inside was a square card bearing an exquisite portrait of four dogs, the black spaniel, the Scottie, a delightful dachshund, and a little hound she hesitatingly identified as an Italian greyhound. On the back was a miniature portrait of eight people. She recognised Gillan and her sons, and the two blonde women, holding their babies. There was also an older man with black hair and an earring, who was presumably the patriarch. He had his arms outstretched as if to embrace the others.

Pip stared at the wealth of detail the artist had got into the palm-sized paintings. Maybe they'd been painted full-size and reduced to fit the card?

She ran her fingers over them and found the surface smooth.

Prints.

A logo on the bottom corner proclaimed that the card came from *Elf-Made Art*.

Pip felt an immediate pang of regret that there were no

similar portraits of the Laurel-Pearmain-de-Leon families. There were photographs of individuals and couples, but nothing depicting them all together in a formal grouping.

Come to that, there were few photos of Pippin Pearmain starring as herself.

She bit her lip, hard, to distract her mind from melancholy.

Then she opened the card.

Inside, attached with a bit of easy-peel gum, was an exquisite silver charm of a puppy.

Pip detached it and fingered it thoughtfully.

Maybe. But what would the cats think?

She bent to read the message. It was written in decided black ink, which reminded her of Cousin Lupin's script. It covered the entire inner surface of the card in writing not much bigger than her own miniature script.

Greet you, Pippin Pearmain. We got off on the wrong ~~paw~~ foot. My son reminded me that we didn't properly introduce ourselves, and if I am to obtain a signed copy of a Juniper Gin novel, which I very much wish to do, I should be more gracious. I should have been more friendly in any case.

Unwarranted hauteur is one of my besetting sins.

If you still want to try your ingenious Dog-Morse experiment on a fay dog, rather than wasting your time on clueless standard dogs and uncooperative muties, I suggest you obtain a puppy and work with her — bitches are more amenable, despite what my husband says — from an impressionable age. If you would like to do this, let me know and I will source a suitable puppy for you.

A heather hoond might suit you, or possibly a harlequin, a holly, or a shadowhond. There are also stable terriers, and various others, but the first three I mentioned are probably the most suitable for living over here. The heathers look as if they'd been put together from leftovers and they're madly enthusiastic. They love everyone. On second thoughts, possibly not the best choice. You'd be forever fielding enquiries as to whatever happened to make your dog look like that. The harlies are dainty and fey and can be small enough to put in a large pocket. The hollies are larger, calm and soothing. The shadows, which I belatedly add to the best-suited recommendation, have the handy talent of not being especially visible unless they wish to be noticed. This might be a tad difficult to explain, but since you already live with fay cats, you will be used to this peculiar attribute. Shadows have good manners. Let me know your general preference.

Like your fay cats, any of these will be intelligent, self-willed, and are of excellent health and vigour. The heather will eat anything not nailed down and dust your furniture with her tail, scattering bric-a-brac and objets d'art in her wake.

I'm not being altruistic. I am genuinely interested in whether this can work. I'm tempted to try it myself, but I think it would be better if you do it. My mutie self might blur the experiment, and you have experience with communicating with your friends the cats. They might even help you to train your puppy if they happen to want to.

You may get in touch with me via my husband's office . . . Branok St Ives . . . or via my personal number which I'll add to the bottom of this note along with an email address.

This offer is valid for the foreseeable future. There would be no cost to you, other than optional reports on your progress and general costs associated with feeding etc. If it's not of interest to you, destroy the card. I don't care for my personal number or this admission of my failings to be bandied about too freely.

Yours in interested anticipation, Gillan Teague St Ives.

"Destroy that card? I don't *think* so!"

Pip tucked it away in her messenger bag, already considering a suitable frame. If she opened the card out so the print was to the back of the frame, she'd be able to enjoy the pictures without exposing Gillan's words to the world.

She'd consider the enormity of the mutie woman's offer at leisure.

Gillan St Ives' claim that her extraordinary suggestion was not altruistic comforted her. She understood acting from self-interest and Gillan was undoubtedly a person who did that. Nevertheless, her son seemed fond of her, so she must have some good points. Her oblique apology to a stranger suggested the same thing—unless it came from a sense of self-obligation.

Pip considered the odd collection of gifts for a while. The apples referred to her name, and the marigolds were a reference to the film Gillan had mentioned. The card was an explanation, and the dog charm a reminder of the offer, or promise, or suggestion.

She shook her head, unable to understand exactly what was going on.

Get a puppy?

The idea was unexpectedly enticing. Holding the little old chihuahua in her hands had offered an odd connection. Maybe she could have the little harlequin. A little dog for a little human. Would that be a cliché? Did she care if it was?

What would the cats say if I imported a dog who has the same provenance as theirs?

She supposed she could ask them. As housemates, they should have a say in who moved in.

She *had* overridden Amberjill's apprehensions in the matter of Lupin's cat, and it had turned out splendidly, but she wouldn't do that again.

She opened the flask and sniffed cautiously. It was some kind of cold drink that smelled of lemons.

Pip grinned as the answer came to her.

Lemon barley water, with lemon verbena. Little Nanna Laurel used to make it.

The napkin enclosed two tarts, one a classic apple and clove and the other a confection with shreds of orange she first took to be marmalade then identified as marigold petals. A leaflet tucked into the napkin proclaimed them of being from *Queen of Tarts, The Belfry, Fiddle Bay*. The leaflet showed a dozen tarts with two of them ticked. *Adam and Eve* and

Marigold Magic.

Yum!

Pip foresaw her regular order from Jelly-and-Juice would soon be augmented by a larger selection of tarts.

At the very bottom of the hamper she found a small book that matched the *Orders of the Fay* series in pattern if not in dimension. *Orders of Field and Forest.*

How had the woman got this care package together so quickly? And why? Was she running some kind of fairy outreach service? It seemed overly lavish for an apology for being standoffish.

She had every right to be standoffish. Pip thought *she* would be standoffish if someone persisted in trying to talk to her when she'd signalled uninterest in socialising. In fact, she often was.

She shook out the lining cloth, realising what it probably was.

Normally, she preferred pink, denim, and green for her clothing colour of choice, but Sulane's thoughtful gift of the rust riding outfit, which she was wearing right now, had swayed her towards the possibilities of autumn shades. The exuberant marigold patterned cloth might do for a shawl of the style Magda wore, or she could have it made up into a dress or a blouse. It could equally be used as a throw over her couch, if Kittisack and Amberjill could be persuaded it wasn't available for kneading or whisker-wiping.

Or a wall hanging. Even cushion covers. A summer spread for my bed . . .

She considered, and discounted, the idea that accepting the gifts would bind her in any way. Traditionally, fairies were tricky, but she'd not come to harm from her recent association with the family at the fossmere. Jisinia wasn't particularly user-friendly, but she was trying to do better . . . as was Jillian Jules. Gillan had proclaimed that they didn't have enemies, which probably true.

She grinned reminiscently at the memory of Pandora's reaction to the mention of her relatives.

Lord save me from Jisinia!

Jisinia was her niece? Therefore, Jisinia's mother or father was a half sibling to Pandora, but no blood relation to Carolyn Hildebrand.

How odd to have a whole other side of the family you barely know. Pandora couldn't even remember the names of two of her nieces and nephews. Or was that an affectation?

She felt her grin fade as envy crept over her.

What I'd do to find some more family! Even if it meant Little Mum or Little Dad had given me a secret half sibling.

She'd discounted her notion of Lupin possibly having a secret child, but her parents were even less likely candidates. Little Mum would never have given up a baby, and if Little Dad had, then Little Mum would have taken steps to have a close and loving connection with that child. Little Mum had been good at unconditional love.

Too late now for family, Pip reflected. She'd squandered the opportunity to stay close with Lupin when she'd flitted to Jellico Bay in 2012, and although she was determined to be a better cousin to Jan and Clarkia, she didn't delude herself that it would make a difference to the eventual extinctions of the Laurel-Pearmain-de-Leons.

Unless Clarkia had a child, the line would end with her.

She closed the lid on the basket and walked out into the middle of the grassy stage.

There was no suitable music, but she hummed "Silk and Circumstance" as she ran through the *dolphins' entry* then the playful dance she'd dubbed *porthole tag*.

She decided her principal dancer's role would begin with a counterpoint. The dolphins could be playing in the sunken ship, and the soloist would be free-diving to the wreck — treasure-hunting. She would join the dolphins. They'd show her treasures they'd found — then the shark would arrive.

Blast, thought Pip. That meant another experienced dancer. By the tradition of ballet, it had to be a man.

She considered the attack. The dolphins could protect the main dancer, but that would lose the pell-mell chase culminating in the transformation into cats.

Maybe I'm looking at this all wrong.

What if the shark is a seafay man after all — not a real one, because I can't imagine attaching one to the production, but a dancer —

A scene leaped into her mind — a chase, culminating in a pas de deux. *The principal wins over the seafay and they go to make peace with the dolphins.*

Next scene, the dolphins transform and dance with the old queen cat, then return to the sea. The two dancers decide to go off together.

Pip took out her pad and pencil again and embellished and summarised her existing notes. Then she contemplated the finished format of her ballet.

Dammit. That won't do.

Introducing a seafay man in place of the shark and using two principal dancers meant the focus would be on the relationship between the principals. That in turn meant the scene with the cats would be out of place.

Pip drew curly brackets around the cat scene and looked at what was left.

Act One. Entry of the dolphins and porthole tag. Delphine arrives.

Act Two. The dolphins show Delphine the treasures. They dance together, and she copies their movements. The seafay arrives. The dolphins flee.

Act Three. Delphine prevents the seafay from chasing the dolphins. She beguiles the seafay in a pas de deux. She considers his offer to *come with me and be my love.* She decides to surface and dances a solo on the shore.

The seafay beckons her . . .

Yes.

Yes.

That might do.

Pip sat on the grass next to the hamper and contemplated her product.

That might work. I'll run it by Jane tomorrow morning before we leave for Delphinium Island.

As for the cat ballet . . .

Pip sprang up and danced the old queen cat. The role came naturally as the queen unfolded in her mind. Elderly but sprightly, slightly sharp, but beloved by all. A wonky matriarch.

She need not give up the cat ballet. She could do that one too . . . it would be a short, single act ballet, and nothing to do with *Delphine.*

Tiny Pippin Pearmain settled cross-legged on the grass again, opened the hamper, draped herself in a beautiful temporary shawl splashed with more marigolds than an apothecary garden, and enjoyed a celebratory feast.

ABOUT THE AUTHOR

Lark Westerly loves writing series where characters weave in and out of one another's stories.

She also loves playing with ideas and notions and researching odd information.

Lark lives in the island state of Tasmania, where she walks dogs, invents recipes, and rapidly reduces her garments to things that need mending. She rarely wears a matching pair of socks.

Unlike Pippin Pearmain, Lark is not tiny, not an only child, not single and not an on-screen performer. She never learned ballet and she can't speak Cat-Morse. She doesn't even have a bucket list. Nevertheless, Pippin Pearmain and Lark Westerly are sisters under the skin.

Oh . . . you were wondering about that bucket that inspired *Performing Pippin Pearmain*? It happened like this . . .

To find out, visit

https://performingpippinpearmain.weebly.com/about-the-bucket.html